Forgiving Us

FLIP KNOX

ISBN
978-1-957895-29-1 (Paperback)
978-1-957895-28-4 (eBook)
978-1-957895-30-7 (Hardcover)

Table of Contents

Chapter 1

"Rehab"

$\mathcal{I}$ am in rehab is not exactly the first line you ever want to read in a romance book, I'm guessing. Yet, here I am. In rehab. I am writing this story on a cheap Samsung tablet with a Bluetooth keyboard, smoking gawd awful half-shine cigarettes, and drinking a cheap imitation coke knock-off. My stomach feels constantly ill, and my body aches. Why? Because I was drinking myself stupid over many things. Surprised I am not a diabetic, nor did I kill my liver.

For three years straight, I have been slamming ungodly amounts of whiskey, rum, and vodka down my throat to blackout, in hopes of never waking up. And for one sobering reason, I finally listened to a friend and checked into rehab precisely three months ago. The clinic is called The Star Program. It's for war veterans to get mental help and treatment for substance abuse. And no, this isn't about a woman I met in rehab. Most rehabs tell you to dedicate yourself to abstinence from romantic entanglements for at least a year. The reason being is emotional turmoil can cause a person to relapse hard.

No, my story is something entirely different. A life lesson worth learning. In pertaining to this lesson, my rehab therapist told me something quite interesting. True love never changes the ones we are with but inspires us to become better versions of ourselves. A man will only change for one woman, not all women. Just like a woman will only ever trust one man and not all men. Love is an evolutionary process in which we change the worst of our aberrant nature to be the exact thing our true love needs. This is why Fredrick Niche once said, "Love is Madness, yet there is a reason for madness."

The side effect of my aggressive alcohol abuse developed something in my brain called "wet brain." The whiskey binges were destroying my memory. I often forget short-term things and even my place in a conversation if my brain is too stimulated. The worst part, my speech can slow down after using the medication they give me to control the alcohol cravings and heal my brain. Being sober is a bitch. One thing "wet brain" can't do, nor time itself can't do, is erase her memory from me. God, no matter how much I tried, by putting a bottle to my lips and pulling the trigger, she has always remained embedded in my soul. I don't know how don't know why.

The only thing I can think of? Love. An ever-crushing constant in the human condition. It is both the bane of my existence and the key to my freedom. Her name? Gwen. Not really. She chose Gwen because most western folks couldn't pronounce her Vietnamese name. As for me, in this long-winded intro, my name is Cliff.

My whole purpose for telling you my story is to hopefully make you: laugh, cry, hope, but more importantly, grow. They say the truest loves only happen once in a lifetime. The one loved one that changes us forever. Some of us get to find this person and hold on to them for a lifetime. For some of us, they are the spark that stirs fires in our souls we will never forget, and yet never get to truly hold. One thing is for certain; it never leaves us the same after.

For me, her memories come like a flooded river. Other times a gentle breath of sentiment. Every time I smell a woman wearing Chanel number five, I think of her. Whenever a unique song comes on the radio that I would typically not listen to, I think of her. Especially the song "Big Jet Plane" by Angus Stone, or more recently, Hiams "If I could change your mind," as it is blowing up in the U.S. for some reason lately, though I heard it with her in Gwen's home country.

Big jet plane was Gwen's favorite song. It clicked for me because I grew up listening to the small town rock of the USA farm town and country music. As I got older, I fell in love with more types of music like metal, rap, and folk. The reason Hiam reminds me of her is because of a funny story.

So for the first time to meet her closest friends, Gwen took me to a mall, and the song was playing. I asked what we were shopping for, and she said quite bluntly, "your dinner attire." Mind you, for this dinner, I did have a smoke jacket, tie, and well-ironed slacks. I was trying to be respectful. Yet, she bought me pair of bad religion jeans and a very tight, form-fitting button-down shirt. One I quit wearing cause I am now fat as hell, and it doesn't fit.

The moment I was going to protest her buying new clothes, she started to dance to the song from Hiam, and it has stuck with me ever since. A confirmation, she called it. That the universe was somehow moving to make me a more well-dressed man, I laughed it off as she danced and sang the song all the way to the cash register. But it was a moment.

The part of the dinner meeting that night gets a little hazy as I look at the old photos I saved and, at times, look at them with a fondness. I remember we went to a cafe where I missed ordering my drink because I didn't understand her country's slang. And I had my first beer at 28 years of age at dinner. The glass was huge too. Aussies love to drink, dear God. What the conversations were, I don't remember. But what I do remember is something powerful.

On the way back to the hotel we were staying at, we stopped at an art museum of sorts. Gwen explained why she didn't understand one artist's body of work as it looks so plain and simple. But my eyes got it right away. The artist, you could tell by his brush strokes, had phenomenal talent. Yet, the artist would strain it intensely, not showing the proper depth of his skill. The artist, for all tense and purposes, was giving us a glimmer of his heavenly talent. This is what kept his admirers wanting more. They could feel the cusp of his greatness and feel it never be fully realized with a great intention. We as human beings will only ever see at times the whims of someone's greatness and never their full depth because we're not supposed to. The divinity of one's human spirit isn't meant to be seen through the eyes of everyone, just the person's chosen few.

And when this moment came as a realization to Gwen, something magical happened I didn't see coming. A kiss from her lips that took the very breath from my lungs made me speechless. Don't get me queer; we made love a thousand times before this moment. But she literally stole the speech from my lips with one single gentle kiss, a kiss I had never tasted before. The kind where you feel the warmth of the mouth, the taste of their tongue is like a gentle exotic fruit you can't make out, and your body shutters from their soul touching yours. Like I said, magic.

You can't fake a kiss like that, as I know she felt it too. It was something real. Something neither one of us had for a very long time. This was how my heartstrings finally understood that she might be worth the tearing and pulling that was to come.

So welcome to my love story, the very thing that has changed my world in so many ways. I am beginning to learn why Ernest Hemingway once said, " the greatest love stories ever written were ones that were truly lived." Because you can not fake real love, you can't conjure passion from an ink pen if you have not felt the fiery furnace of passion. Nor could you ever understand the most genuine depths of the human soul in poetry if you have never made love to a person where you literally feel their soul breathing in and out of your lungs. So every love story, a truly great love story, has a deep level of many truths, as does mine.

Some of these writings will not be precisely true, as these are my therapy writings in rehab, and I don't want to discredit any person. But I did truly love Gwen, and since being here, this place has allowed me to put into perspective what we were. The hard thing for me, though, is, I don't know if she did love me. Caring for me deeply, I am sure she did. But love? I may never know. But this can be my cynical nature as when I do think of her from time to time. I knew Gwen did best by her actions and crazy ways. Though at the time, I viewed her ways as extravagant.

Chapter 2

"Writing Therapy"

Dr. Remy is a unique woman with a unique worldview. She defies most clinical expectations and pays close attention to our true person to understand us more and to call us on our own bullshit. She does not believe in over-medicating a patient and refuses to treat patients as if they actually matter. She was pissed when I first entered rehab that my old psychologist just signed me up for a pharmacy distribution center full of meds and said he would check in on me every few months. I was so heavily medicated I couldn't sleep, making my PTSD worse, and gained new symptoms as side effects of medications interacting with other medications badly. It's scary how lost in the shuffle veterans get at the veteran hospital.

This is why I like my therapy time with her. Plus, she is a therapist that doesn't shy away from things too easily.

It was 9 a.m. when I was given this writing assignment from her after she put me in my place a bit. I entered the room around 8:05 a.m. and waited for her for a good ten minutes, I think. When she came into the room, I knew she had a plan for me; I didn't know just for what. She kept the small talk, short and sweet, all the while sharing her genuine smile. But what I didn't realize was she was coming in with an arsenal of questions to break down and explore who I was, which she had a deep idea of already. Basically planned a resounding round of verbal jujitsu to back me into a therapy process fit for my true self.

"So. you're a writer?" she asked.

"I dabble," I replied.

She then shook her head and began to scroll something on her computer screen that I couldn't see.

"I find you a fascinating person, Cliff," she laughed gently, "in your file, it reads you are a construction worker for Adli's road crew. Yet, during group therapy sessions, I heard you quote Geoffrey Chaucer subliminally. From his body of work, "The Canterbury Tales," to be exact. You kept it real subtle too. You didn't do the posh thing and quote the author or the book you referenced, and you blended the sentence in with the point you were making. Just like a philosophy teacher would to a class full of students. "

"All I did was read the book in high school and didn't want to come off as arrogant," I told her. "It became one of my favorite books my high school made mandatory reading, especially the short story inside it called, "A Knight's Tale.""

"You are very good at distancing yourself with half-truths," she quipped back, "but I am no longer going to accept that here."

She had me, and I knew it.

"High School students may like a required reading text," she said, " I liked Beowolf. My brother was fond of Macbeth. But no one pristenly quotes a text and hides in plain conversation. And it's not the first time you've done it either. You have quoted Dante's Inferno, numerous quotes from the bible in modern English, and even checked a book by Rober Frost, a famous poet, from our Library."

"So, I like to read books," I scoffed

"huh… Lucky for you," she smiled as she leaned in, "I checked your military record. You earned a degree in world philosophy and associates in world literature. Why lay asphalt for a living if you can make more money, doing less backbreaking work?"

"Philosophy people don't tend to make $48 an hour," I quietly quipped back.

Which is when she finally swung her monitor around to show me what was on it. My stomach sank, and I felt my heart leap into my throat. Somehow Dr. Remy found my old blog where I wrote poetry and tiny stories about Gwen. The particular one she had up was after Gwen and I first met called "Love & Stale Coffee." I could feel my hands shaking so bad I had to grab my armchair rests.

Upon seeing this, she flipped the monitor back around.

"Nothing is more tortuous than knowing true love and losing it," said Dr. Remy, "did she pass away?"

"No," I said.

"The reason why I ask this," said Dr. Remy, " your body is showing extreme signs of a panic attack usually associated with a bereavement response. So, she was your world at some point."

"What does this have to do with my healing doc'?"

"A soldier is struggling with moral conflict with what happened to the war, who: never smoked, never drank, before almost dying twice from both his deployments, found peace after seeing such evil. Peace in a woman who held his heart in the palm of her hand, and when that failed, it was the straw that broke the camel's back for him," she told me, "he no longer cares about being in the gym. However, he used to be very athletic and now lives in a small desert town where no one knows who he is exactly as his family lives in other states. His house is a one-bedroom double-wide with a solar panel roof and cool wall heat paint. In a small town where no one knows who he is."

"How does my house factor into your analysis for treatment?" I asked her.

"Have you had sex in the last three years?" she asked back

"What?"

"Have you had sex within the last three years?" she asked again, "It's a simple question."

"What does my sex life have to do with that I live in a trailer?" I replied back

"Answer my question, and I will answer yours."

"Yeah. With strangers mostly. People I'll never see again," I told her, still very confused with her line of questioning.

"Yet, they never were once in your home, were they?" she asked in a gentle voice

"No," I replied. "Mostly a hotel room."

"A safe distance of social intimacy," She said as she sipped from her coffee cup," you never go to their place of residence, nor do they go to yours. Just a carnal act of existence with no way of actually getting to know someone or someone getting to know you."

"Still doesn't answer how my sex life and my home life are related to my healing process," I replied.

"You got a single bedroom double wide, painted with cool wall heat resistant paint, and a solar roof," She said as she placed her coffee mug down gently, "Signs of not wanting people near you. "Cool- Wall Heat Resistant" paint protects your house from rotting from the heat; solar panels make sure you don't have an electric bill, which means no meter man comes to step on your property. And your double wide is essentially a car you can sleep in that can't be renovated to add a room or two, a strong sign you don't want anyone in your life, which is why you moved to a small town to put your trailer home. A sleepy town that has nothing going on. I bet the only exciting thing that happens in your day is when you go to the post office and might to give someone a polite gesture, as you pick up your mail. Yet, your body craves sexual attention because, for a brief moment, you feel good. You have become a man who gave up so badly; you hate human interaction even though you crave it so much."

She could see right through me. As I said, she called us on our bullshit. The truth is, I gave up on people and myself. I did not just long for death. I welcomed it with open arms.

"How many sexual partners have you had, and how many were paid?" She asked me next with deep concern.

"I don't know," I said as I held my head in shame. I began to feel her line of questioning, bringing small tear swells in my left eye, so I did my best to wipe it before she could see.

"This is a safe place, Cliff," She said, "I don't care if you had more sex in the last three years than a drunk college student on spring break. I need to know where you are. This program only works with absolute truth. This is how wounds heal, and you progress into a healthier version."

She paused for a long while and let me gather my thoughts, and then let me speak. God, that pause felt like an eternity.

"Ok, so what do you want to know?" I asked her

"I have been doing this for many years and seen many men and women walk in here just like you," She said lovingly and sternly, "she was a party girl before you got with her, right? Sex with different partners and probably used controlled substances?

"yeah."

"Yeah, what?"

She gave me another long pause to let me breathe.

"Yeah, she used cocaine habitually," I told her, "She couldn't turn down a good party. And her "friends" would, at times, spike her drinks for a good laugh. But I suspected more."

"So you fell in love with an addict," She said

I couldn't say anything. All I could do was nod my head yes.

"It's quite common actually," She told me.

"What is?" I asked

"A soldier was falling in love with someone they want to save after war," She replied, "that never asked for saving. The problem is, you see the real person, and yet, you are punishing the real person for what the addiction did to you. This is going to be a hard road. A walk through hell, unfortunately."

"So, what do you want me to do, doc'? I asked as I wiped my face with a shirt collar.

"Have you ever seen the Notebook or read it?" Dr. Remy asked me.

"Yeah, have a good memory with Gwen on that, actually."

"Good. Then we can start there."

Dr. Remy got up and went to her walk-in closet in the back of her office. When she returned, she gave me this Samsung tablet and keyboard I am writing this story on now.

"You know how the main romantic lead built his lover a house?" She said, "Same idea. You are going to write a Romance book about Gwen. I want you to focus on the love you two had; tell me everything. Use your love of poetry, philosophy, and writing, to make it the best romance story that you can."

"And what would be the point of this?" I asked.

"You need Al-Anon therapy, along with treatment for your alcohol abuse and PTSD," She said.

"What's ALANON?" I asked, genuinely curious because I had never heard of it

"A therapy system that helps people heal from the traumatic experience of loving someone with a deep addiction," She said, " Right now, you are viewing her character through the lens of her addiction trait. I need you to analyze the truth of the love between you and her so that you can forgive her and yourself the horrors you both did to each other because of her issues."

And just like that, I was given a path to explore my way to freedom of the self-destructive life I was living. The reason the character in the Notebook built a house, was to build a house for the love of his life, though they fought so much. Dr. Remy's idea was to use my talents to really explore who Gwen was, and the good things she actually gave me, and explore our connections to where pain could be forgiven.

So per my assignment, next chapter, I am going to share my Notebook memory about Gwen to explore the good nature of her. The only weird thing is, I have been instructed to also explore deeply in my writing, the nature of our love making. In which I kind of understand.

Gwen was a partner like no other. Gwen's sexual apitite was different than mine, and pushed my boundaries. As I did grow up very strong in my faith, and it is my faith that made me view sex a certain way. That was until I fell in love with Gwen. Gwen had the power to take me to the full exploration of sex, and passion, that I thought I would never do. I would just get lost in her, and let her drink from my soul until she had her fill.

And it is the extreme nature of sex I followed Gwen into, that I feel heavily guilty for, at times. Was the wild sex life I went through with her, truly Gwen trusting me and wanting to explore crazy ideas and wild things, because I was partner she trusted? Or was it a weapon from an addict to make me think our love was deeper than it really was?

Chapter 3

"Island Marriage"

The most incredible night of my life came in the spring of 2015 when Gwen flew in to see me while I was living in Hawaii. We got a spiritual marriage by Island Shaman near a secret place locals don't usually allow outsiders to visit. However, this sweet man wanted to bless us, and we wore rings made of driftwood after. So I wanted to make our night special. Something Gwen would never forget. Also Gwen was a devote Buddhist, and I was a Christian struggling with my belief in God at the time, so doing this, this way, was us compromising on what we wanted our marriage to be.

When we got home to my apartment, Gwen headed into the shower, while I proceeded to set the mood. I lit small white candles around the living room and kitchen area and laid a duna cover on the floor in front of the tv. I laid a small batch of rose petals on the blanket to make it look extra special. Then I ordered the movie, The Notebook on the streaming service I was using at the time.

When the mood was set, I began to prepare food I knew Gwen would enjoy. Simple stuff, really, a salad that used fruit and wine vinegarette, topped with blue cheese crumble. But then, when I poured her favorite wine, which was called "Pig in the House" (a very dry red wine), my world was brought to its knees.

All I heard was, "Are you ready, hubby?"

And when I turned around to see Gwen, my heart began to beat through my chest. There she was, standing in something I wasn't ready for. I knew Gwen was into kinky stuff. However, knowing her sexual appetite didn't prepare me for this night. This night is forever etched in the memory of my heart.

Gwen wore black eyeliner to draw my eyes into her. Her bleach blond hair was down and straight. She was wearing a soft choke collar made of lace on her neck. Her corset had lace patterns that showed some skin areas, where, when seen, hinted of completely exposing her breasts or parts of her back. She wore a leopard print thong to draw attention to my favorite part of her body, her ass. She made sure it was a small fit to her curvature, too, so as to make her ass look bigger and expose the area on it where she had tattooed my name. Her high heels were black with bits of yellow to match her panties.

I wasn't ready for Gwen to show her true nature to me. My hands started shaking so bad I had to place the wine glasses on the counter in the kitchen. I tried my best to play gentleman, preparing the dinner plates.

"I have your favorite movie queued for you while we eat dinner," I told her

But Gwen had different ideas. She walked up to me slowly and began to kiss me like that night we stopped at the museum. Every kiss made me weaker than the last. I could feel my hands having a mind of their own as my fingertips traced down her back to the crack of her cheeks as her hand found its way to unzip my pants.

As she began stroking me gently, she pulled back some and made sure I could see into her eyes.

"Silly boy, you are the meal for dinner," She said.

Then my body shook as she bent to her knees and placed me into her warm mouth. My left hand couldn't help but place itself onto her head to help it slowly rock back and forth, making me feel in control.

She was very good at making me feel important powerful. As she knew my body was beginning to come close to a climax, she ensured her throat could be felt with my tip. And I began to release; my legs began to buckle to where I could no longer stand on my own. How her small 80-pound frame had the strength to finish me and hold my then 164-pound frame, I don't know.

Without saying a word, when she was done finishing me, she began to crawl away from me in a manner to allure me for more. I was lost in her.

As I began to walk towards her, my clothes seemed to fall by the wayside, in the path to her destination; the cover with rose petals.

She stopped and stayed in a pose of all fours and stretched her arms out to the floor until her breasts were on the ground and her ass was arched just right.

"Now give me your mouth," she said.

And before I knew it, my tongue was buried deep inside her. I was licking, sucking, and nibbling.

"Both holes, god damn it," She moaned.

So I obliged. From her crack to her vagina I was lost in the tastes of her—a sweetness. A flavor I cannot explain. It was like something I never had before her, nor have I tasted anything like it after her. Giving her oral was like nothing I had ever tasted before in my life.

When I was erect again, in the passion of the moment, I ripped her panties and shoved myself deep inside her. The louder she screamed, the harder I would thrust into her. Then her body gave a sign that it got what it craved. I could see her body going limp as her mouth bit into the cover. Then her body fell to the floor and gave small shacks. Gwen has been satisfied.

I unzipped the back of her corset to take it off and just lay next to her. Her hair smelled of coconut oil, and her smooth skin smelled of Chanel Number 5.

We laid there naked in the warm candlelit silence for a good moment before she reached for the remote control and played the movie.

Now I usually hate romantic movies with a passion. But, this night was different. My mind was open, and I was willing to learn about her world. Every so often, she would pause the film and explain why that particular scene always grasped her heart. She was teaching me her soul.

When the movie credits rolled, we paused for a moment, and we locked eyes in a way we never had before. A way that made Gwen hide her face from me for a moment.

Knowing the romantic moment was over, I went into the bathroom to brush my teeth first, and she then followed suit after. She thought we were going to bed right away, as she got in the bed covers right away.

However, my heart was not yet set on it. My heart was heavy from what happened three weeks before Gwen flew into town to see me. I knew she felt it.

That's why she asked, "What's wrong, hubby?"

I paused for a good while, I admit. Let the tension breathe somewhat in the room.

"Gwen," I said, " My heart can't handle you doing drugs anymore. I just can't. I know I might lose you tonight for saying this, but I am in love with you, and I'm scared."

I could hear the tears run down her face as she began to sniffle a bit. She breathed in deep a few times and then spoke

"Ok, hubby," She said. "I promise no more drugs."

At that moment, when I turned to her, I don't know what drove me to make the choice I did. I slowly stripped the covers off her body and got on top of her, and placed myself inside her.

My thoughts knew, for some profound reason, she had wild sex, good sex, bad sex, and sex on drugs. But I felt as if someone had never made love to her. I looked her deep into her eyes, saw her vulnerable soul, and worshiped her with human dignity. And I swear that night, I could see her real soul in her eyes.

At the sweet moments when we kissed, my cheeks could feel the tears that ran down her cheeks. Her eyes not once could move away from looking into my eyes. And when my body began to finish, her hand, in a desperate motion, grabbed my ass and forced me as deep as I could go inside her. All the while, her gentle eyes never moved off my eyes.

It was like the moment we sought love; love sought us and began to save something in her that I had no idea she had lost.

We love the things we love for what they are. And that night, I was her husband, and she was my wife. Her eyes told this truth.

When it was over, my body couldn't help but slump over on the bed and pass out.

The next morning, when I woke up, she was lying there. Her eyes were wide awake and excited to see I woke up next to her as if she finally found something.

I don't think I'll ever forget that night.

Chapter 4

"Midnight"

It's midnight, and I am already burning through my ninth cigarette. I am currently struggling if I should let Dr. Remy know, in retrospect, the full details of that magical moment in Hawaii. Or rewrite it with a personal story that has less meaning only because the gentleman in me doesn't like the idea of kissing and telling. But my heart is also telling me she needs to know. So this writing is me meeting her in the middle. I am not a coarse pig or ill repute bastard who lives for the desecration of women. I just happened to fall in love with a woman from a different country who migrated from another country, who had a different worldview than my American one.

It reminds me of a conversation I had with a French woman and Matt Daigle of Top Brand Entertainment comics. Matt fell in love with a non-American woman who lived a different social life than most Americans.

Backing the story up a bit, I am an avid comics books fan. I didn't learn to read like most kids, so my brother taught me how to read through comic strips. This way, I could visually see what the words I was reading meant by how the character was drawn. As I got older, I started reading graphic novels and my English teacher Mr. Carter took notice. And he opened my eyes to something powerful. The great comic/graphic novel writers I was falling in love with, Alan Moore, Grant Morrison, Niel Gamien, Chris Claremont, and James O' Barr, were doing something unique that most don't see. They were teaching literature, poetry, and philosophy through storytelling, just like the religious writers of the Bible, Quran, and Torah.

It's an ancient writer's technique that very few use today. The last person I read who uses this technique is Paulo Coehlo.

Mr. Carter gave me a book to study called "The Divine Rule of Hermeticism," which explains this ancient technique in great detail. How stories influence our lives, and to teach someone something powerful, teach them in a story. This is why I fell in love with Philosophy. Philosophy is wisdom wrapped in poetic words through stories people can relate to—basically the art of teaching profound ideas through entertainment.

Chris Claremont did this with NightCrawler, a Marvel superhero who looks like a demon. Yet, he wants to be pious and be a Priest. NightCrawler is then chased around by the town folk believing him to be a demon, and the town folk tries to kill NightCrawler. Why is this impactful?

According to comic legend,Chris wrote this story during the '80s, the height of the Aides scare when Americans called Aides the Gay disease. You had many gay folks of various Christ-influenced institutions such as Baptist, Catholic, Mormon, and so on, being vilified by the very same people they called friend or family. Which helped move a subculture in America, where gays invented a hidden way of talking to each other to avoid persecution going on at that time. So Chris, being a very educated man filled with compassion, wrote this story based on inspiration from real-life events and wrapped it in allegory as many gay folks were having a crises of faith due to them being hated for being different.

Which is why I laughed as a teenager watching conservative media types get so angry that Alan Cumming, an outspoken gay actor, played NightCrawler in X-Men 2. NightCrawler was made as an allegory for gay rights initially. Which is why I am at odds with the new NightCrawler writers in the direction they took the character.

The new writers of NightCrawler don't know the characters' history. They take the fact he is a Catholic Priest or a Christian Monk of some sort and uses his religious belief as a valid reason for the character now being homophobic. I can see why modern readers who grew up with NightCrawler as an allegory of a gay person struggling with a crisis of faith hate the character's direction in current continuity. Not understanding the character's old history is alienating its original core readers, who then vilify it, driving away new readers.

There is a reason every X-Men movie came from Chris Claremont's writing. Chris wrote the X-Men book title for 20 years, and the reason he was able to do this was he was able to teach deep thoughts that connected with readers.

Writers today don't do this. They do what's sensational for emotional response.

So, back to Matt. I was at a comic convention where I talked with Matt and a French woman who wanted to be a writer. Please don't ask me her name, I can't remember. I just know I used to pen pal Matt back when google plus was a thing, and we talked comics. Any who, she asked an important question to Matt:

"I want to write a comic, but what I want to write, I am afraid Americans will find it crude," She said.

"What is that?" Matt asked.

"Genuine sex and confidence of human nature," She replied.

Matt laughed and understood where she was coming from. Matt then grabbed his graphic novel series The Swingers and gave it to her.

"Yeah, Americans are weird when it comes to sex," Said Matt, "but if it helps, I have written this exploring different viewpoints on sex. And yes, it does get graphic."

The French woman's eyes grew wide with excitement as she found an American understanding of where she was coming from.

"Yes, exactly," She said, "Why are Americans so uptight about a woman's nipple. I have one, and you have one. In my country, and the neighboring countries, breastfeeding in public is ok, and video games like Grand Theft Auto are outlawed."

"I agree!" said Matt, "As I get older and work with more European creators, I think we as Americans might have it backward. I got a graphic novel for adults inside a popular chain in America, and I asked them, are you sure it's ok because, in one scene, a guy is lobotomized with a hammer and a screwdriver by a serial killer. What if a kid gets to it? And the buyer literally said American parents don't care about kids seeing violence anymore. And he's right. Do you know how many kids are playing war games and crime games where they are slaughtering people? Yet, American adults are not ok seeing breasts."

"Sex is natural," said the woman, "When I crave it, I get it. If I have a child, I will feed it from my breast. But I would never let a child ever play such a violent game or allow murderous movies on tv being played around any child in my home. I just find it odd Americans vilify sex and glorify violence. People get horny naturally and sleep with a person they enjoy. Violence is something unnatural. That's why so many people are broken after war."

"Which is also why my best selling book, Swingers," said Matt, "sells in great numbers in other countries but America. I agree with you, and I think we have it backward in this country."

Now, keep in mind this is a blip of a conversation. And it is from my outside looking in point of view. Where you land philosophically on this point is your choice. But as I told this part of my life story, it does open up why am I so nervous sharing the most magical moment of my life in great detail?

Is it because human beings are highly judgmental creatures to where we punish ourselves for not wanting to fall in societal standards or something else?

Truth be told, I have had wild moments in my life before Gwen. And because of my old beliefs that I was raised with, I did crucify myself for them.Yet, when Gwen asked or just starting doing something I couldn't say no. All Gwen had to do was whisper in my ear or touch me with her finger tips and I would be so lost in her that it wasn't logical.

Gwen hid the fact she did coke, and other drugs for two months until I visited her in Australia for the first time. Why did I not hit the road once I found out? I don't know. I saw the danger signs, and the train wreck coming, yet, I walked right into that storm. Truth is, no one could make my heart beat the way she could.

When I was in Gwen's bed, it felt as if I was the only one who existed. And when Gwen and I would spend all day on the phone or on skype, it was like the world didn't exist outside of us. Yet still, in all that warmth and love, I could feel I was losing myself. And for every good heart warming moment that made my world turn, I have memories that are a wicked hell to remember.

I have memories of Gwen where my brain hurts in the back of my skull. Where my heart races so fast it begins to knock the air out of my lungs to where I find it hard to breathe. My body begins to sweat, and shake. It is like as if my body is terrified of Gwen and wants to run from her memory. And the only way I found that stops those deep dark moments of Gwen was drowning in whiskey hoping God wouldn't wake me the next morning.

I know addicts play emotional mind games to get the high they need, but I thought the pain from that would stop once Gwen and I were no more. And yeah doc', I will admit it here as I couldn't choke it out in therapy. I did seek the comforts of women for 6 months after Gwen and I ended when this feeling got too bad. Most the time during this time it was paid for as I didn't have to talk with or play a flirtatious game. All I know is sex made the pain of losing Gwen stop and the whiskey killed the guilt after.

I never thought I would lose myself like this.

But then their were some dark times that I did stuff with Gwen where I know her addictive side corrupted our marriage bed. I just saw how much pain was in her soul and I wanted it to stop. And when I complied, Gwen didn't go out for a high or a binge. So I did whatever I could to try and save the woman I called my wife.

I would've gladly walked through hell if it meant for just one night Gwen was home safe. Which is why some nights I hate her with such a deep aching passion. And some nights, she is the greatest love that I'll never touch again.

Song I listened to while writing this:

"I been doing things that are bad for me. I been going to places I shouldn't be. I been getting high and staying up for weeks. I been doing things that are bad for me. I been getting high and staying up for weeks. I been doing things that been bad for me. To make me feel better. To make me feel."

– Peter Raffoul "Bad For Me."

Chapter 5

"Therapy to Trust"

This morning after writing the last three "Chapters," I had to give my writings to Dr. Remy. I was nervous. My heart was beating through my chest, and my lungs felt like it was hard to breathe. So, when it came to my therapy session at three in the afternoon with her, my stomach tied in such a knot I wanted to vomit.

The very moment I sat in the chair in front of her desk, Dr. Remy gave me the tablet back with the keyboard.

"I knew this was the right therapy for you," Dr. Remy said with a smile, "How did it feel, slipping back into the memory of Gwen as you were writing it?"

"Good," I replied.

Dr. Remy sat on top of her desk in front of me and leaned back a bit like a teenager would.

"Not a good enough reply," said Remy, "what did you exactly feel when you were writing that story of Gwen?"

"My brain felt warm, my heartfelt calm," I said

"Were you finding yourself aroused?" Dr. Remy asked

"Yes, why?" I laughed nervously.

"Even better," Dr. Remy said, as she leaned forward as if to look me deeper in the eye, "I promise I will tell you why I asked that after you answer me this. What happened three weeks before that powerful moment? In your writing, I can feel how traumatic it was for you. What did Gwen do that made you stop and say no more drugs?"

Dr. Remy let me have a pause of silence and gather my thoughts as my eyes teared for a moment. I took a deep breath and began to speak.

"We both heard about a bad string of cocaine killing folks on the news," I told her, "Drug dealers were cutting it with meth and a date rape drug. Some people were taking it and dying. Some people were buying coke just cut with a date rape drug so that they could have fun at another's expense."

"So naturally, your protective nature was trying to help her how?" Dr. Remy asked.

"When I called her that night, I told her not to go to the party that night, that I was worried," I said, "maybe this one time just, don't go out. Just to be cautious."

"And she freaked out on you, didn't she?" Dr. Remy asked

"Yeah," I said, "We got into a huge argument. Gwen was screaming and yelling, and I- I was begging her not to do it. So, she said, fuck you, and broke up with me over the phone. Before she hung up the phone, however, she did say something truly nasty."

"Which was?" Dr. Remy asked.

"You'll want me back. They all want me back," I said softly as I felt anger build in my chest.

"Calm cliff," said Dr. Remy, "that was just her addiction, not her. What happened next? How did you two reconcile?"

"Well, a few buddies called me up to go bowling, like, right after," I told her, "and while at the bowling alley, my anxiety was through the fuckin roof. I kept thinking I might wake to a phone call that she would wind up dead. So, I cut out early. I tried calling her at least, what, a hundred times, I think? Every call is straight to voicemail. Figured she blocked my number."

"Go on," Dr. Remy instructed.

"I got home, and I called a mutual pen pal friend," I told her, "someone we kind of met together in person and told her the story. She tried calming me down, and in a fit of my anxiety, I did something very stupid. I took my sleep medication I was prescribed at the time and popped them like candy while shotgunning shots of whisky a buddy left in my fridge from a barbecue, and I hung up with her after twenty minutes. I know it was stupid doc'. I just never had that kind of anxiety before where my brain felt tight, and I just wanted it all to stop."

"You were trying to commit suicide," Dr. Remy said.

I paused again for a long while and cried a good cry for a good minute. Then I gathered my thoughts, and Dr. Remy started again.

"So, how did you survive?" asked Dr. Remy

"Two of my buddies knew something was off," I told her, "I used to leave my apartment unlocked in Hawaii cause it was on post. I felt no need to lock the door. Cali, my one friend, found me in my kitchen and dragged me to the bathroom after realizing what happened; and placed my head on the toilet and started putting his fingers down my throat, making me vomit. Gains, my other buddy, called 911. When I sobered up, I don't know why the doctor of the hospital never reported it, nor did my friends ever talk about it."

"Doctor may have thought of an accidental overdose," said Dr. Remy, "common thing in military hospitals. And why didn't they report it? Most civilian doctors find military laws and regulations too strict human nature."

"Yeah," I said.

"So how did you two reconcile after?" asked Dr. Remy

"Midday the next day, Gwen called me," I told her, "she was distraught and begged me to forgive her. I don't know, doc'. I never thought I'd fall in love with an addict, you know?"

"That's why ALANON therapy systems exist," said Dr. Remy, "loving an addict can be very traumatic to lovers, parents, siblings, and children. So traumatic, in fact, the sober person in any one of those roles can become controlling, manipulative, or self-destructive as they begin to feel the addiction was caused by them, for some reason. I am going to hold off telling you why I asked why you got aroused by writing about Gwen."

"Ok, why?" I asked curiously.

"Because I need to know more of your sexual history," Dr. Remy replied, "because reading about how you described Gwen, you knew she had a dark fetish side. That Gwen liked to dress up and possibly entertain certain things in the bedroom you weren't used to. Yet, she drew you in with no hesitation. So, what did you do that was abnormal from your small town Christian upbringing before Gwen started showing this side of herself?"

"I don't know?" I told her, "Well, I do; I just feel nervous telling you."

"Try me," said Dr. Remy as she crossed her legs and sat up straight on the desk as if she was ready to meditate.

"I had two friends with benefits before her," I said, then paused again, before continuing, "I shared a sexual partner twice with a friend. Both times are very different, and with different people."

"There it is," said Dr. Remy, "go on, tell me about them."

"The one was a friend I flirted with in Korea," I told her, "She was our barracks manager. One night, we had a party in the barracks, and she hooked up with a buddy I deployed with. Then, she knocked on my door, and had sex with me too, the same night. We were drunk off cheap wine. The other time, it was more of a threesome. A friend said she was happy to be back from deployment and wanted to get laid. So we went to a house party together, and she hooked up with another guy and me. Again, drunk off whisky that time. Still friends with both, they send me Christmas cards every year."

"There it is," said Dr. Remy as she got off the desk.

"There it is? What are you talking about, doc'?" I asked, perplexed

"The beginnings of your risky behavior," said Dr. Remy, "there is a reason why every medical visit asks about how much do you drink, do you wear condoms during sex, or have you paid for sex. Soldiers who survived hard deployments need real human connection. And sex indistinctively provides that level of connection. Alcohol just lowers the inhibition; you were all going to have sex regardless; alcohol just made it less restricted. You had a beer with Gwen, but it didn't stick. Whiskey, vodka, and rum are party alcohols of combat soldiers. It's possible your heavy drinking started to be developed during deployment parties. Feeling good, celebrating you are alive. Which also led to risky sexual behavior. There is a reason every military base in the world, doesn't matter which country it belongs to, have long streets filled with bars, strip clubs, and brothels."

"Ok, how does this help me out," I asked

"You learned social behavior to self medicate with booze and sex from a war soldier mentality. How long that would have lasted, is anyone's guess. Some soldiers go through a phase, some don't do it at all. And a small few get lost in it," said Dr. Remy, "one of the major factors in war soldiers divorcing spouses is the spouse feels like the war veteran's sex drive is too much, while the veteran thinks they are not getting enough. Hyper sexuality is very common in both men and women who served in war. Did Gwen have any family members who fought in Vietnam?"

"Yeah, her uncle," I replied, "Gwen's Uncle joined The Navy Seals for the Americans."

"Did the Uncle go to brothels and drink with his war buddies after the war for a period of time?" asked Dr. Remy

"Actually, yeah," I told her, "Gwen grew up thinking it was ok for men to once a month go to a brothel and drink with their buddies. Well, that was until Gwen saw civilians having normal marriages."

"So, Gwen knew something you didn't," said Dr. Remy, "Her Uncle's war struggle taught her unhealthy coping mechanisms soldiers go through and Gwen's Aunt allowed it until it burnt out, Gwen probably was . Soldiers long for deep human connection after surviving a horror story. Sex releases in a person the same chemicals in the brain as the chemicals of a woman holding a child. Sex is a safe place. And trauma, fear, regret, are why mothers hold children. Your body is designed to look for things to help heal itself. So finding yourself in a woman's bed when the pain hit too hard, should not be villainized. Nor should you villainize Gwen's behavior either, because there is a lot of trauma, guilt, and shame that goes into creating an addict. Deeply traumatized people latch onto sex because the body wants to heal."

"Yeah doc', I get it. But what about vets and people who can't be touched or lose sexual desire after war or a traumatic event?" I asked because I was curious.

"Trauma is like holding two beer bottles. One in each hand," Dr. Remy said, "You take them and drop them both on the ground at the same time. One bottle completely shatters, and is useless. The other breaks half way, and becomes a weapon to harm oneself, or others."

"What about when the sex I had with Gwen gave me full blown panic attacks?" I asked

"What kind of sex are you ok with?" asked Dr. Remy, "Some like it dirty, some like it safe. What is normal to you, the way you are built?"

"I understand love making," I said, "or having sex in public for the thrill of almost getting caught. I am ok with sex can be wild where it's fast and hard. Hair pulling, ass smacking. Times when a lover left scratch marks on my back or a bite mark on my shoulder. But…"

It was in this moment the panic attack started to happen. The back of my brain feeling tight. The heart pounding so hard against my lungs I couldn't breathe. While my body began to heat up to the point I began to sweat heavy.

Dr. Remy gave me a pause and kneeled before more, and grabbed my hands in a prayer like caress. Dr. Remy then gave me time to calms down, and then made me look in her eyes as tears formed under them.

"Gwen was into a sexual life you weren't expecting wasn't she," Dr. Remy said, "Cuffs. Ropes. Rough stuff. Things of that nature?"

All I could do is shake my head with a gentle yes, as I couldn't speak.

"Was Gwen the dominant or submissive?" Dr. Remy asked

Again, I couldn't find the words nor the strength to speak.

"Gwen liked kinky things that morally pushed your boundaries, didn't she?" asked Dr. Remy

I gathered all the strength I had to gently nod my head yes as tears began to fall from my face. Dr. Remy then gave me a moment, and after, used her hand to wipe my tears. When I was done having my moment, Dr. Remy then sat back on top of her desk.

"Gwen probably was always this person," said Dr. Remy, "and probably opened it up to you cause you were her husband. Gwen didn't use the sex to break you, she was trying to be herself in your marriage. It was make believe, it was playing around, fun in the bedroom that should have been safe. But, what should have been a married couple exploring sensations of sex and pushing one another's limits, was hell for you because you saw real harm and real violence in the war. So any act of bondage sex triggered you. Yet, it was this kind of sex Gwen craved when she wanted to get high. So it was either, fuck me, or let me get my high the other way."

Again I couldn't say anything, just sit quietly.

"So you did what she asked," Dr. Remy continued, "like a fireman running into a burning building. You would have sex in Gwen's way, and then when she realized you were triggered, she would sex your way?"

"Yeah," I admitted

"Gwen being a wild woman in the sack isn't terrifying or wrong," said Dr. Remy, "Gwen just wanted her husband to enjoy her bed. Likewise, you must have loved the hell out of her to put yourself in that kind of torment so that she wouldn't use. Proves you are a good man, though you don't believe it. Good men go through hell for the woman they love. Bad men would have used Gwen's wild side to hurt her. And sad to say it, it probably has happened to her. And being a man who was sexually and emotionally manipulated, it happens with loving an addict. Gwen the person is trying to be herself, Gwen the addict just wants to feel high and will do anything to get that high. It's like loving Dr. Jekyll and Mr. Hyde. But for you to be manipulated by Gwen's addiction this way, reveals something powerful about you, Cliff. Do you wish to know it?"

"Sure," I replied

"There are four types who join the military in any country," Dr. Remy said, "For some it's a family trade. Some are poor people needing a good job, and military service provides: clothes, food, a warm bed with a paycheck and benefits. Then you have the evil bastards who want the legal means to kill someone, who can load a rifle pull the trigger and not lose a nights sleep. Then there are the noble, the protectors. The people who join to protect life and innocence on the battle field. The ones you come home when the war is over and have to deal with the seeing the dark side of humanity, when no one else would. And because you would rather suffer than have Gwen use drugs, tell me you are the noble kind."

She paused for a moment as she pondered on something before speaking again, but excitedly, "I don't think you are ready to know what I am doing or know what comes after we explore this trauma from Gwen in full detail. I want to tell you. It's like wanting to slip from my tongue, but we need to go deeper. I need your help to explore your past more. So, I have an assignment for you."

"Ok, doc'," I said, ready to know what she wanted me to do.

"Write about this encounter with us, then when you come back for your therapy session tomorrow," She said, "then write how you met Gwen and how the relationship started between you two. Then, in therapy, we will open it up with you explaining how one of your friends with benefits started, and I will show you something about Gwen you didn't analyze yet.

"Ok, doc'," I replied.

"Lastly," Dr. Remy said, "you never told Gwen of the suicide attempt, did you?"

"No."

"I see," said Dr. Remy

She nodded her head in silence and let me leave her office with the tablet and keyboard.

Fuck, this therapy idea is weird.

Chapter 6

"First Times"

Technically I met Gwen on social media. I didn't meet her in person initially; I really didn't know her, know her until we started texting each other online. She liked a few of my posts now and again, and I would like hers. But nothing crazy. I never slid into her DM's unless she texted first. I just wanted to be a proper man.

The night she and I woke to our crazy love affair was just after she disappeared offline for a few weeks. She came online, and we, for some reason, started texting none stop that day with short texts. What's your favorite movie? What's your favorite song? And so on, until I asked, "Why did you disappear for a month?"

Gwen texted, "Went to a meditation retreat to get grounded spiritually."

That night, I hosted a small barbecue at my place and let people unwind. The work week was long and brutal, so friends needed a place to blow off steam. I have been doing this now for two duty stations up to this point. Once a month on payday, give people the free room to pop off.

A safe place to eat, drink, or hook up with a lover if needed. No fundamental standing rules; just don't be an asshole. And I only ever invited people I truly trusted. Why? Because I came up in the Army when don't ask don't tell was still in effect.

A rule that basically discriminated against gay servicemen and women. Meant, folks couldn't ask if people were gay, nor could gay folks come out as gay. Because if you were found out to be gay, you could be punished under military law. And I had a few gay friends who I deployed with, a safe place to be them. A place where they could love, be loved, and their lifestyle accepted.

My thinking was, "I could sleep with anyone I wanted with no recourse, yet, they were willing to die for me, and they couldn't enjoy who they wanted to sleep with? That's not fair."

So, I made my home a haven for the outcast and rebels, which in turn gave me a solid, healthy, weird family dynamic of misfits and rockstars.

Come to think of it; I think this was the first night I tried fireball. I must have taken; God knows how many shots.

When the party wound down, and two friends were sleeping in my spare bedroom and another on my couch because they were too wasted to drive, I shut the lights off and went to bed.

But as I lay there for some reason, I checked on Gwen's social media feed for some reason. She and another girlfriend were telling dirty jokes, and this guy was being kind of creepy, trying to talk dirty with them. For some reason, I texted on her post-

"Playing on words, Shakespeare would be proud!"

Gwen then texted, "Oh, how so, Mr. Gentleman?"

I replied, "You two are purposely texting each other play-on jokes about masturbation and ignoring the horny creep in the comments section as a joke to get a rise out of the poor bastard, and the dumb fool can't even see it."

Needless to say, the creepy perv guy blocked me right away. Which, in my tipsy moment, made me laugh.

A few moments later, if not seconds later, Gwen texted in my DM's

"So, how did Shakespeare play with his words?"

So I went, full nerd.

Notice that text she texted, and I'll come back to it.

I texted, "Well, in Macbeth, the main character calls his stepdad the word mother. Implying the man was a motherfucker."

A full minute went by, and Gwen texted, "you don't flirt with women often, do you?"

If you are laughing at this hard, I get it. To be fair, I was intoxicated. Her text was flirty with another masturbation hint, but this time aimed towards me. I was stumped and starting to sober up, as she was now gaining my full attention. So sat up and watched her give another response

"Come on, don't be shy now," she texted.

I replied, "A gentleman is never shy; I am just waiting to see if a lady is truly ready."

"Then how did he play with his words?" She texted.

"Not like how we are about to, I imagine," I replied back.

A long pause came, and after something, I wasn't expecting.

Gwen sent me a photo of herself completely topless, with her panties showing as her sweatpants were pulled down somewhat.

"You don't have to imagine. I'll let you see it," Gwen texted back.

So I did what my horny mind only could think of. I texted her pictures back of my six-pack and chest muscles.

Then I texted back, "I'll go only as far as you want."

Gwen then replied back, "show it to me, unzip your pants, and show it to me."

So, I did.

She then texted back, "thank you, baby," as she sent me multiple photos of her topless in her pink panties. They were bikinis; from what I could tell, I wasn't too sure, nor did I care.

We just started masturbating to each other while texting what we wanted to do to each other.

The fantasy was this:

She would come into my room and kiss me deeply. Then as my body would relax on the bed, she would begin to place me in her mouth and suck me nice and slow, making me feel every inch of her throat.

I then would pull her off and place her on her back, kissing and sucking down her neck, while my fingers would slide gently down her panties to rub your vulva gently. My tongue would trace itself down her neck and find her breasts and suck them slowly yet firmly. As her hips would begin to thrust my hand, I would kiss down her belly until my lips could taste her panties. I then would take off her panties with my teeth and place my tongue deep inside her.

"Would you bite me good, nibble my cherry?" she asked.

And so, I would. Not hard, just something to make her thrust her hips into my face while grabbing a fist full of my hair. If she was going to give me her body this night, I was going to touch her in ways she needed.

When she was good and ready, I would slide myself deep inside her. Thrust into her as hard as could, make her feel every inch of me. And when her body begins to tense up in a way that would lead her to scratch down my back, that's the sweet spot I'd make her remember me. Because I always love watching an aggressive lover's eyes roll back into their head or give that look of sweet embrace that the climax is coming.

So when I would see that divine moment in the eyes of Gwen, I would lower my shoulder just within her orgasmic reach and let her bite as hard as she needed. The intensity of her love bite would tell me when she wanted more and when her body would have enough.

Because when her sacred moment would have come, I would have flipped her over onto her shaking hands and knees, placed myself inside her, and got mine. I would go as hard and fast as I needed to get mine in return.

All Gwen asked for was that I would pull her hair. And I would have. At that moment, I knew I by the way she texted that she had a wild side no lover really saw before, yet, I said nothing. And I was right about it too, cause later on in our relationship, Gwen allowed me to know the real her.

I don't know that night; I just knew something deep about her. As if I knew her deeply before this moment. Yet, I held back, and let us finish together, and let the moment be the moment. I had never sexted before that night, so it was all new to me.

We both logged off after, and I couldn't go back to sleep. I was wide awake. I must have stayed awake for an hour or so before I emailed her something I thought a gentleman would email her. So, I went to her profile, copied her email address, and did just that.

The reason for this was my grandfather raised me to always be a gentleman after being with a lady and to make sure you take her to breakfast and buy her favorite roses or flowers after. If the lady turned this gesture down, it's ok. But you always offer every time.

So my email read:

My name is Clifford William Hetfield. I use my nickname in my handle as most people call me by my nickname, and it makes it easier for friends and family to find me when googling me. I don't know why you chose me tonight, but all I can say is, thank you. I needed to be seen by somebody. So now you know something true of me.

It took a whole day to get an email response back from her, and her reply was:

"Thank you for this. When I woke up this morning and realized what happened last night, I was going to block you. No joke, I had a long conversation with a friend about not sharing nudes with men, and I did last night with a stranger. Call me when you get the chance; I want to hear your voice."

So, I waited a few hours. My mind was racing if I should call this woman, whom I didn't know, yet, just had cybersex with. But the moment came when I was jogging; my brain just stopped me dead in my tracks. I opened the messenger side of the social media platform app I had met her on and called her.

When she answered, "hello?"

My immediate response was, "YOU'RE AUSTRALIAN?!"

She then busted up laughing so hard I could hear her snort.

"Oh my Gawd," Gwen replied, "I jerked my cunt to a yank. Well, I guess this app doesn't inform you about where others live, aye? How's it feel getting in the knickers of a woman halfway across the world?"

I had to laugh. It was just crazy.

We started out as online friends with benefits if we came home with no one to sleep with. I know my love affair with Gwen started crazy, was crazy, and ended crazy. She was just something in life I wasn't expecting.

Chapter 7

"The Truth of Writing"

So today, after writing my last chapter, I met with Dr. Remy about five in the evening. I gave her the tablet and keyboard sometime after breakfast, and this time I didn't feel anxious over it. However, I was a little apprehensive about our meeting. I wasn't sure I wanted to go into sexual detail about my first friend with benefit. But then again, writing this stuff out and talking about it did lower my guard in opening up about my suicide attempt.

This time Dr. Remy was wearing yoga pants and a t-shirt instead of her usual business attire. Her desk was removed from the room for some reason, along with the chair I sat on the session prior. In their place were two yoga mats precisely 7 feet apart from each other.

"My fat ass ain't doing yoga doc'," I said

Dr. Remy laughed and shook her head.

"I bet you used to when you cared to be healthy," said Dr. Remy, "I looked up some of your old profile pictures on your old page. 165-180 pounds lean muscle, six-pack, with broad shoulders. That took a lot of training."

"Well, I'm not a soldier anymore," I replied

"True," She noted, "but that's not why you let yourself go this bad; we already distinguished that a few sessions ago. No one gains 30 pounds, quits shaving, and dresses like a hobo because they get out of the military. You're purposely making yourself look horrific as a protection mechanism. Lay on the mat, and close your eyes.''

"Ok," I said, "but why are you dressed like you are about to do yoga and have two mats then?"

"Because I just got done doing yoga and didn't want you laying on my mat for fear of ringworm," She said, "I'll explain the reason why I want you laying on the mat after our therapy session."

So, I obliged Dr. Remy, laid on the yoga mat, and closed my eyes,

"So," She said, "you are still deflecting and denying why you let yourself go. And though you are looking unattractive on purpose, you still manage to have sexual partners. Which means there is something about you that you are purposely hiding."

At this point, I took a deep breath because I knew she had found another piece of me I didn't want to share.

"After reading your last few entries, I got a theory as to why," Dr. Remy said, "I reached out to the friends on your call list that you provided to the program in case anything happened to you. And I asked the one who cared for you the most as to why you had partners attracted to you, though you let yourself go. You know what she said?"

"No, doc', I can't read minds," I told her. By the way, laying on my back with my eyes closed, I felt kind of stupid.

"He has the ability to make anyone in a room or conversation feel as if they matter," said Dr. Remy, "that you focus on conversations and interests of the person, to make them feel like you are actively listening to them as no one else can. Not many people have that skill, Cliff."

"Where are we going with this?" I asked

"You'll see," Dr. Remy said, "Now, focus on your first friend with benefits. Why and how did you become that intimate, but not intimate, that you two became an item?"

"She just got out of an old-fashioned relationship she felt was making her feel claustrophobic," I told her, "and I just got back from deployment about two weeks prior. She was a single mother, and I just started renting a condo on my own as I just made E6, so I was authorized to. I told her to bring her kids over, they could play video games, and she could teach me how to make lumpia."

"So, did you really want to learn to make that food, or was it a guise?" Dr. Remy asked, sounding a bit sarcastic.

"No, I am a huge foodie," I told her, "that's why my old social page has pictures of me barbecuing and cooking random stuff. I like learning about food."

"Ok, go on," Dr. Remy told me

"So, I let her kids play video games on my PlayStation while she taught me how to make Lumpia. My phone was blowing up with texts from a fashion friend I met when I got back, who knew I knew how to airbrush paint on human people."

"Why do you know how to do that?"

"I used to do cartooning, and when I would go to comic conventions," I replied, "I saw people that liked cosplaying, and so I learned how to do body painting as a way to make extra cash. So, when my friend found this out, she asked my fashion friend to help make her look like some comic character. So she gave my fashion friend her measurements and then asked me to help find body paints that matched her skin tone to match the comic character green skin, without making her look hideous."

"So what did you do?" asked Dr. Remy

"We stopped cooking, and I took her to the garage of the condo where I had my airbrush painting stuff," I said, "I showed her before, during, and after paint job photos of clients I did in the past. The next thing I know, she is stripped down to her underwear, and I am testing paint colors in contrast with her skin. How we started having sex, I don't remember. But she was bent over my art table, and we enjoyed a quickie. We then cleaned up, made dinner, and they all three spent the night at my house. I slept on the couch while she and her kids slept in my bed."

"She snuck out from the kids a few times away from the kids to have more sex with you, didn't she?" laughed Dr. Remy

"Yeah, of course," I said in frustration, "how is this helping me heal, doc'? What age of wisdom are you getting out of my old hook-up?"

"You confirmed what your friend said was right," Dr. Remy said, "a single mother who leaves a man she felt controlled by, wanting to feel sexy, needed the attention of desire. She wanted to be freer with her body, and here you are, not judging, giving her the path to do so. So, she, in turn, gave you what you needed."

"Ok, so how does that relate to Gwen?" I asked

"You both have social similarities," Dr. Remy replied, "but are you seeing patterns yet, between Gwen's life and your own life?"

"Gwen went away for a period of time, and I gave her sexual attention when she came back," I told Dr. Remy

"Exactly," Dr. Remy said, "a psychological theory on human nature is we are programmed by the company we keep, and we attract people in our lives that are programmed to think like us, most of the time. Soldiers coming back from war often drink and have sex to celebrate living. When Gwen came back online, you reacted like the culture you surround yourself within the military, and the way your grandfather raised you, is why you had to ensure she felt like she wasn't being used. You needed to be a gentleman. In other words, show me your friends; I'll show you your future."

What Dr. Remy said, seemed to make sense. Not saying a BBQ with friends is bad, just that I possibly allowed the culture around me influence a weird decision.

"Do you want to know why I had you lay on the yoga mat now?" Dr. Remy asked me

"Yes," I told her.

"I am using your cognitive bias to help you," She told me, "most war soldiers from your terms of deployment hate meditation and yoga because you had to sleep on mats like these. As anything that feels, smells, or looks like something from the war makes you feel uncomfortable. It's not because you're unsafe in your body; it's because your body is conditioned and trained with certain things, and now those certain things serve no purpose for you, which allowed me to control how happy your little man in the tent might become, as you talked of an old lover. There is more going on, but when you are ready, I will explain."

This was when it started clicking for me, seeing the method to Dr. Remy's madness. I was learning truths of my past I didn't see, and Dr. Remy was walking me through triggering things that could have caused a flashback from the war but did it in a way that the flashback didn't happen.

"Last thing," said Dr. Remy, "before you leave this session, was the reason why Gwen went to her meditation retreat, to help her get sober?"

"Actually, yeah," I told her, "her sister put her in a 30-day program to meditate, eat clean vegetables only, and learn to love herself because her cocaine use was getting out of hand, and a few other reasons. I didn't know that, though, until much later."

"I see, Gwen basically just detoxed," Dr. Remy answered back, "then let it be a warning, and hopefully something to help guide you. Thirty-day programs usually never work. Six-month programs usually work because it's when the real person reawakens in the individual, and they see how the demon of addiction is ruining their life and controlling them. That's why one-year programs work best. The real person is back and in control of their own mind and is able to see how to have a healthy relationship with other people."

Then it hit me like a ton of bricks to where I had to ask Dr. Remy, something the program warned us about in the beginning.

"Wait," I said, "Is this why all the doctors strongly suggest not having any romantic relationships for the first year of sobriety?"

"Yes," said Dr. Remy, "it's to save someone from hurting themselves and others. If not, it is like an atom bomb waiting to explode, and it hurts many people in the process. Gwen got clean for 30 days yet never cut her party friends out and got romantically involved with you, which is why your relationship ended with her, truthfully. When a person is unhealthy, they make others unhealthy they get involved with."

After Dr. Remy dropped this truth bomb, all I could say was-

"Fuck."

"Now our goal," said Dr. Remy, "is divorce your anger towards who Gwen actually is and place it on her demon of addiction. This way, you learn to love the real person of Gwen from your past, without giving her the halo effect, and learn to forgive her properly. Because I truly believe, without a doubt, you two loved the hell out of each other."

"What makes you believe that doc'?" I asked

"She tattooed your name on her ass, and after she left," said Dr. Remy, "you gave up. Which means it is possible, she too, is struggling with things about you. And though you two are no longer in each other's lives or ever see each other again, we can heal some of the hurt. And with your writing, help you build a metaphoric house to her heart, where her memory won't haunt you but give you closure. Because what I do know about life can be summed up in three words: life goes on."

"You quoted Robert Frost," I said, almost cutting her off.

"Yes, yes I did," Dr. Remy laughed.

"So how did you know I loved literature and would quote when I talked?" I asked because now I was curious.

"You write poetry that explores deep thoughts in your off time from therapy. The staff have noticed it. And so I started paying attention to how you talked," said Dr. Remy, " That and you sketch people you observe. Which indicates you are very romantic soul. Which is why I chose this writing therapy for you. I want you to channel your story of Gwen through writing like other war veterans did before you as writing seems to help people process heart break. Ernest Hemmingway struggled with what he saw in war and struggled with a love affair which he used to inspire a brilliant love story called "A Farwell To Arms." However, to connect with your nerd side, Jack Kirby the man who created Captain America and most of modern comic characters, channeled his trauma through his artwork in comics, inspired by the works of Van Gogh. Tolkien vented out his war experience and the longing to be united with his love in writing Lord of the Rings, while Ian Fleming created James Bond's dark sense of humor to help process the horrors of a man killing another man such as soldiers he served with did. But I don't think using an allegorical story like Fleming and Tolkien did will help you. I prefer you write a memoir that will explore Gwen and your struggles with her. Continuing to write about Gwen will allow you to process her, and guide you to forgiving her. And when that is achieved, we can do the next step in your therapy to help you process parts of the war you don't want to talk about."

"ok," I said for confirmation

"Hemmingway is suspected to have channeled his greatest love affair with Gellhorn through two books. But don't mask what happened in allegory like Hemingway did, but give the truth. Tell exactly what happened in a poetic way. However, I want you to start using one of Hemingway's writing tropes as you write," Dr. Remy said, "Or at least, try to."

"Which one?" I asked.

"The woman of light, and the woman of darkness," Remy replied, "Gwen is your woman of light, yet, her addiction and the people who drive her to use, is her woman of darkness. The difference between you and Hemingway is-"

"He was a better writer than me," I said, cutting her off with a smart-mouth joke.

She laughed and, after a moment, regained her composure.

"The difference is, Hemingway used this trope possibly to purge himself from the guilt of cheating on his wife," said Dr. Remy, "While you are going to use this trope to forgive your ex wife, Gwen. Gwen was Buddhist, so write the light and dark trope of Gwen from the yin and yang perspective. You are a great listener, so this time, it's time for you to really listen to Gwen's story from the worldview she held."

"So, which Gwen story do you wish me to write now?" I asked Dr. Remy

"The part where though you were worlds apart from each other," said Dr. Remy, "you had to come together and experience each other in the real moment, and what happened the first time you both met."

Chapter 8

"In Transit"

I guess, to start this part of the story, I need to share other things. For a few months, Gwen and I video chatted with each other and talked on the internet messenger every day. And yes, we even got intimate through skype calls. It was the only way we could see each other and, in our way, touch each other. I never fell in love before, really, so this was all new to me. I still don't remember how we became so foolish to date each other over the internet, but it was something real. As hard or as weird as that sounds to explain, that was the truth.

We developed something intimate between us that, for the life of me, I don't know how it started. But our choice of intimacy caused a great rift that almost made it to where we couldn't see each other.

Every morning when Gwen woke up, she would text me to ask me what color of underwear to wear. I would text her back the color I would like to see. She would take a couple of photos, front, and back. Then she would send the photos to me before she went to work, so on my lunch break, I would get them. It was our thing. It made me feel important and wanted. Like I got to know something intimate about her and make an intimate choice for her that nobody knew about. Why she did it every morning actually, I don't know. I thought she was doing it out of love.

Anyway, we were planning on her flying out to see me first. I was getting my house ready and buying foods and wines she liked, you know, to give her a good visit. Unfortunately, one weekend, something horrible happened. While visiting her sister, Gwen let her older sister borrow her phone to take family pictures. And when her older sister did, she accidentally swiped over one too many times, and she saw one of the pantie photos Gwen had texted me.

From there, the nightmare snowballed. I guess Gwen's older sister thought at first I was some perv that was going to use Gwen's sexy pictures to blackmail her because she was famous. Which was not true, I didn't even know who Gwen's sister was until after the incident, and even then, I had to google her, no joke. And during the conversation, Gwen mentioned that I had been an American soldier. Let's just say it was over for me in Gwen's older sister's eyes because Gwen's sister not only hates Americans but deeply loathes American soldiers.

To be honest, I wasn't there, so I don't know what was said. I just know from Gwen her sister said some hurtful, hateful, and derogatory things about me because I was an American soldier. Never had some person hate me, even though they did not know me; it was weird.

In fact, before Gwen and I had our magical night? Gwen showed me the texts her sister texted her before she flew in to see me. They were horrific. But something was off about the writing I couldn't explain, So I asked Gwen to save them for me and text them to me. It was like they had a rhythm and purpose with them. Hard to explain. I'll share what possibly was going on before this chapter ends, I promise.

So, after that weekend, Gwen told me everything that had happened with her older sister. And for a while, things got strange. We didn't facetime as much, we didn't phone call early in the mornings, and we stopped sharing intimate stuff over the phone. I asked if her sister was causing this, and she said no.

Later, when I saw her in person, she did confess her sister set a challenge to see if I was true or not, and she put our love to the test. At first, I was agitated; she lied to me, but I let that go. Cause in my heart, I felt I needed to prove the negative wrong.

So, I bought a plane ticket to fly to where she was—that simple. I even booked a hotel for the week I would spend there, a nice one. One that had room service, if I wanted it. When I did this, I texted her the dates I was coming to visit her and the hotel I would be staying at. This way, if she really did love me, she had no excuse not to see me. I wasn't going to her house, and I wasn't asking to visit her family; I was just asking for her time.

Gwen was ecstatic when I told her. For two months, we over-planned everything, just like high school kids. We planned at least a month of things to do in one week. What shows we would see, what foods I would try, hell, even how many times we were planning to have sex. In fact, we even planned, and this is no joke, what clothes I should bring to wear for every occasion to match her outfits. It's what kept my heart going when I knew Gwen's sister was being too intrusive.

Then another unexpected thing happened. While at work, a ground chainsaw I was using with my crew broke. When it broke, the chain that held its dig points together snapped, and one of the screw points flew out of nowhere and hit me in the testicles. The worst pain I have ever felt in my life. I was rushed to the hospital in a quick hurry by my foreman.

While in the hospital to be seen by the doctor, Gwen freaked out. She texted a whole bunch of times-

"What's going on?"

"Are you ok?"

"Baby, what's wrong?"

"Please, I know what my sister has said hurt you. Please don't give up on us."

So, when I texted back on what happened, she rang up on the phone right away. I could hear the "thank God" in her voice. So I was given 21 days of medical leave with pain medication and fancy ice packs to rest my testicles with to not be in so much pain.

So to not get fat, while on medical leave before my vacation to possibly meet Gwen, I ate nothing but vegetables and drank water for 21 days. Why? Well, I was raised Christian, Baptist to be precise. In the bible, Daniel fasted for 21 days against an evil king by eating only vegetables and drinking water. So as my communion with God, I did the same. Good or bad, I wanted this life experience with Gwen.

So, I talked with Gwen when she called and watched Australian tv shows and movies to learn, or I should say, attempt to understand, Australian culture and customs of what Netflix had to offer at the time, which wasn't much. I mean, at this point, I didn't know if Gwen was going to show, and I prepared my heart for the reality, Australia was going to be a nice tourist visit.

What kept me solid in that I was going to see Gwen though, however, was something small and insignificant to most people, but it gave my heart the little extra it needed at the time.

On day two of my 21-day medical leave, Gwen facetimed me after a month of not doing so. And there she was in a lovely flower dress and asked if we could eat dinner together and watch the same movie together. Because Gwen lived out in the country, she only had the movies she owned because a streaming service ate up too much of her data. And I had only Netflix because I was a blue-collar worker who worked 15 hours a day; I didn't need that much tv in my life.

The movie that she owned that happened to be on Netflix was a gift from God. A miracle of epic proportions. She owned "A Knight's Tale" with Heath Ledger. When I found it on Netflix, I could feel the disappointing whimper in her voice. Gwen must have bought it for her two boys. What I didn't tell her, however, was and has always been my favorite film. Like I said, a gift from God.

I made my vegetable medley, and she poured herself some soup, and we watched the film. Here are the reasons I fell in love with this beautiful film. I understand how people dismiss it for a plethora of reasons. But hear me out.

My favorite line in the film is "Change your stars," it's repeated in 100 different ways. It's about poor folks not liking where they are and changing their position to get a better life. This is the mantra of Americanism. Poor people can come here, work hard, and no matter what, change their stars for the betterment of their families. The dream we Americans wish for every poor person. I know the dream is far from reality, but we need to believe in dreams to change the world.

Second, the old-school rock music just makes the film absolutely fun. I love all kinds of rock music, what can I say?

Thirdly, it has some deep historical value to it. When watching the film, it is easy to miss specific historical accuracies in the film because most don't pay attention to history class in high school. Will is a poor man who falls in love with a rich woman in the movie. He is so poor he doesn't understand the proper social etiquette of things of his time.

For instance, Will follows his beloved into a church on a horse, and once the church folks realize it, there is a horse in the "House of God," and Will is promptly chased out of the church. Why is this unique? All Will cared for was his love and became a blind fool to seek after her, yet was denied, which is a common theme in Christian writings dating back to the 16th century for one. The truth was, only the rich could tithe in those times because only they could afford to. The political and religious systems in those days were so corrupt only the rich went to mass/church. And Will, like Jesus Christ in the bible, mocked this system of unfairness by his presence chasing after love.

The film's villain is a pious jackass persecuting Will, as the pious jackasses in the bible that killed Jesus. The villain quotes the bible with the bible verse from Daniel 5:27, which reads, "You have been weighed, you have been measured, and you have been found wanting." The reason this is so significant is only the rich in the knights and kings days could read the bible as education was expensive. Plus, the villain was miss using the verse to toat his own prowess.

Another thing. The dress scene. When Will's true love asks what color will be wearing at the dinner dance, Will's friends say green. Which in medieval history shows he's poor. Rich folks chose blues, purples, and Reds. Green and brown were for poor people's colors, as green and brown were easy to make. Meaning Will's love knew he was lying about being a Knight and loved him anyway. Proving love does not care for: money, politics, or religion. Love wants truth and equality for all; that is it.

Lastly, and most importantly, it is about love. Will is fighting for love in its true form against religion, politics, social status, and wealth inequality.

So Gwen and I are fighting against the world (or so I felt at the time) and watching this film? The evening just felt right.

Then, another gift from God happens. I watch Gwen spray her perfume on as she asks me my favorite pantie from her underwear drawer so far. And so I tell her a certain black one. Then she asks me for my address and if I like tea, as she has only ever seen me drink loads of coffee on skype. Then she asked if I had ever tried Vietnamese candy.

I should have put two and two together, by the way, after her questions and what came next, but I loved her and just wanted her attention.

Gwen continued to FaceTime after the movie was over. And at some point when I was so into the film, Gwen had removed her flower dress and was in nothing but a bra and my favorite panties on. Now I was still in severe pain like no other, so sexual desire was far from me. But my heart melted deeper into who she was. She was trying to give me a night of all about me.

Six days before flying out to see her, I received a package. It was from Gwen. Inside the box was: Australian candy, Vietnam candy, tea, and of course, the favorite panties I had seen her wear sprayed with her favorite perfume, Chanel number 5.

Which is why I got on the forbidden plane of love against logic, to fly halfway around the world to see her.

For the uncomfortable part about Gwen's sister's text, I am just not ready yet, doc', it's too weird. Give me some time, yeah? I'll finish writing about Gwen and I's first initial meeting in her home country tomorrow, as it's Saturday, and I'll have extra time. This is a lot to explore, doc, but I have a funny feeling your weird method is working.

So, chapter 9 will be more about what happened when I met Gwen unless you don't want me writing anymore after what I write on Saturday.

"Final Boarding Call"

To say I was nervous boarding the plane to see Gwen is an understatement. Just before getting on the plane, I was on the messenger app with her, and she asked what color I wanted her to wear, so I told her black. And during that long 14-hour plane ride, all that was on my mind was"

"I hope she kisses me right away."

and "I wonder what black pantie she will be wearing just for me."

And not once did I ever think:

"She's going to stand me up."

or "I am being played.

Though I should mention avoiding currency transfer prices from a currency kiosk and going through the headache of calling my bank every other day to ensure they knew I was in Australia so as not to lock my account, I loaded a prepaid visa card with $3k in Australian currency before leaving the U.S. Which turned out to be way cheaper by the way than going to a currency kiosk or ordering cash in Australian currency from my bank for the trip. Now everyone uses cards and cash apps, so preloading a prepaid credit card isn't a life hack anymore. But back then, banks were trying to make money by converting currency.

The most interesting thing about my flight was I booked with JetStar. Jetstar was a budget airline, the first time flying on one. Uncle Sam usually covered my travels and booked me on normal flights. I was shocked when I got the tickets for $300-400 bucks, but during the flight, I understood why. On a budget airline, you pay for all the comforts on the plane at an exorbitant price.

Luckily before getting on the plane, I ate a small breakfast and bought some sleep meds. This way, I could just sleep on the plane and be somewhat ready to go without too much jet lag.

The plane landed, and I got off. Australian customs escorted me to a secure room because my passport alerted them that I was a prior service member transitioning out of the U.S. Military. My job from the military fell under the awesome geneva convention code where other countries Armed forces and or Secret Service Agencies get to tell you where you can and cannot go in the country you are visiting. Plus, they like to remind you which country because of your code you can never visit for work, play, or general travel, such as stopping in said countries for connecting flights to go to another country unrelated to any of the countries I am barred from.

Not to be an asshole about it, however, but like, 60% of those countries on my do not visit us list, I have no desire to ever go to. I don't feel like visiting places that might make me disappear in a horrific fashion or be snatched and grabbed for ransom money. This is real life; Jason Bourne and Jack Reacher do not exist, for they are male-orientated masturbatory superhuman fantasies that cannot and will not exist in real life.

Though I am sure, the actors who played those roles gave many women who watched them shower nozzle material for weeks just by taking off their shirts.

Then, I walked out into the common pick-up area. And what happened next, I found interesting to me.

"Hey, hubby," Gwen screamed from across the way.

She had to do it twice, however, because her voice in person was a higher pitch than on telephone calls or phone apps. So that's when I learned the communication devices we use would lower or higher our normal voice pitch.

I wonder if this is why movie stars sometimes go unnoticed in the street? Because the audio they record for their lines in get's E.Q. to sound pretty to our ears, yet, that might distort their natural speaking voice. So if a sound person puts more bass in an actor's voice, and all you ever did was watch them in a movie, we might miss them due to not hearing their voice through an E.Q. output, but rather, their normal voice output.

I'm sorry, I trailed twice now.

The first thing she did was grab my bags before I got to the pick-up area. It wasn't hard to see which bag was mine; I still spray painted my luggage with my name, like you're trained to do in the military.

Of course, she kissed me and took me by the hand to lead me to the cab she flagged down.

Now my testicles hadn't healed completely yet, so I was still taking the painkillers the doctor gave me. I took one on the cab ride to the hotel, as I thought we would drop my bags off and go for dinner, which meant a lot of walking. So I didn't want to be in terrible pain, and I took it to ensure I wouldn't be limping all night.

We checked into the hotel I booked and placed my bags and her overnight bag in the closet next to the bed. Once I locked it and walked towards her, I was given the shock of my life.

I was never expecting to be body-slammed onto the hotel bed as if I weighed nothing by a 5'8 (175 centimeters), 80 pounds (36 kilos)woman. And before my brain could register what was going on, Gwen was on top of me with her crotch pressing against mine.

"Alright, yank," Gwen said, "let's see what you are really packing, aye?"

And before I could say anything, I finally got to really feel what it was like inside her mouth. The way her tongue ring felt when her head slid up and down my shaft. The way my tip tickled when it touched the back of her throat every so often. Then, when I was good, hard, and ready, she moved her panties to the side and put me inside her.

After a brief moment of Gwen riding me, I saw her eyes roll to the back of her head and fall to the side, as her body tightened in orgasm. We had been texting sexual stories to one another, building anticipation for weeks and weeks. So, when she finally got to experience me, it was like an orgasmic explosion.

The sexual tension we built up must have felt like masturbating with no actual payoff, and now at this moment? That payoff finally came. Looking back, I think that is why women like reading words from men, such as novels and poetry. When a woman is romantically swooned by a man, her brain is primed for absolute pleasure to where when they get it from the one they love; the orgasm is body convulsing. So after realizing this, I damn sure I always mentally stimulated Gwen with romance every moment I could.

The shock in her eyes was beautiful, though, even when I couldn't stop laughing. It was just a life experience I didn't expect.

"You tell anyone of this, you're dead!" Gwen said while laughing.

I don't know why she got a little embarrassed after, or what anyone does. It just means the person you are with knows how to excite you really well.

That night at dinner, as we walked to this famed place in Sydney called "The Rocks," Gwen kept taking pictures of the night sky as it changed colors. She was like a child with a camera as she fell in love with how quickly the sky colors could vary from gold to reds, and a few shades of purple in between, in mere seconds. Honestly, it was her love of nature that helped me develop a reason to stop and look around in life once in a while.

At dinner, my body was craving sugar badly. Because my injury made me stay home and not work out or be active, I had only eaten vegetables and drank water for 21 days. So, when I saw the dessert menu, I ordered my food like an 8-year-old. Gwen laughed so hard.

While Gwen ordered a salad and a nice classy meal, I ordered a meal that should have put me in a diabetic coma. I ordered pancakes with frosting, chocolate chip sprinkles, a s'more milkshake, one scoop of ice cream, and a piece of cake for dessert.

"Do you always eat like this?" Gwen asked in amusement.

"Oh, no," I told her, "only when I have trained really hard or been on an extreme diet does my body crave something this extreme. One year after training for the Boston marathon, I had an Army physical test after the event, about two weeks after. Before the test, my body was craving salt like you wouldn't believe. I should have just poured a salt shaker in a cup of water, to be honest."

Gwen laughed.

When the food came out, I was weirded out a little as Gwen kept moving things around the table.

"What are you doing?" I asked

When Gwen realized what she was doing, she stopped, hung her head kind of low for a moment, and then fessed up with what she was doing.

"I'm sorry," Gwen said, "just my ex, the guy I dated before you, was a terribly messy eater. So when we go out to eat anywhere, I rearrange the table in a way that makes it impossible for him to spill anything."

All I could do was laugh. We all had lovers of the past that gave us bad habits of some sort that made us look crazy on first dates.

My weird quirk was after eating; I stacked the plates properly to help make the clean-up neat, orderly, and easy for the kitchen staff. I developed this habit when I worked at a diner for four years in high school when dating a waitress. Gwen liked the idea.

So, when we got back to the hotel room that night, things went a little slower. Gwen went into the shower to take a rinse while I put on romantic music in the likes of old folk songs and soft rock songs.

When she came out wrapped in a towel, I knew it was my turn to shower, and so I hopped into the shower, in which I laughed to myself a little bit. Here is why.

Most Asian women I had dated while in Japan, Thailand, and Korea, showered and made me shower before any adult fun time took place. I was on a 14-hour plane ride from the U.S. to Australia, and Gwen just ravished me with no thoughts of cleanliness. And now, we were doing things the proper way all of a sudden. I guess.

When I got out of the shower, Gwen was laying on the bed naked, in an enticing manner. Lights were turned down low, and the soft music continued to play.

I don't know what it was about her, but not once did I ever think of using a condom. I had to taste her, really feel her, and breathe her in. I was incredibly nervous; my body shook as I slowly climbed into her. Gwen's fingertips set fire to my soul as she traced them gently up and down my back.

We became a tangled web of human flesh, swimming in a sea of sheets. I was intoxicated by the coconut oil in her hair and the warmth of her tongue tracing my body everywhere.

As the slow passion of our bodies started soft and learning of each other's special places, within an hour, it turned into a lustful fire of need and want.

Gwen's hands loved to scratch my back when I thrust in a good spot that made her thighs shake, and at times before I climaxed, my hand would grip a fist full of her hair, proving I was claiming her that night.

It was my first marathon sex moment in a long time. I never pulled out when my body needed to release, nor did Gwen want me to. Gwen made it clear that night as the passion got more intense, either I was to finish inside her or she was going to swallow me.

And in between those divine moments, as I tasted her sweet sweat on her skin and felt her body flow over me like a wild river, Gwen's sweet Angel lips would entice me with new position ideas or scream her favorite curse word when she climaxed.

That night I tried anal sex for the first time. Gwen had coconut oil, and it was an experience. I was scared cause no woman I had ever been with ever enjoyed the thought of it. But here was Gwen, priming me with coconut oil, as she bent over before me.

"Go slow, at first, hubby," Gwen said

So I went slow. Very slow. Until I heard Gwen start moaning faster, that's when I realized Gwen was using a vibrating ring on her finger and pleasing herself with her fingers simultaneously.

This time, I was going to pull out, and as I did, Gwen did something I never saw coming. Gwen jerked me until what I had to release was all over her breasts. After this, I was spent, my body collapsed in exhausting defeat.

My body, after that, drifted in and out of sleep. I remember Gwen wiping me down and tucking me in before showering to rinse off her body.

I slept like the dead. My body didn't wake up until I felt Gwen's head slide from my chest down to my thighs and place me in her mouth. I couldn't help but wake up then.

Gwen made sure this happened around sunrise. The reason was Gwen wanted to be adventurous and have sex on the balcony while people were running around below us not to be late for their jobs. It was like she loved the thrill of almost being caught if someone would just slow their life down from the rat race for one moment and lookup.

Gwen, at other times, is not like this at all. Gwen, at other times, is very, very, reserved. When Gwen feels caged or imprisoned to an idea or structure, she needs a sense of absolute freedom.

Freedom for Gwen, at times, is like a drug that soothes her soul.

Which again is why we had sex on the balcony. It was unconventional. Oftentimes looked at as poor taste or purvey. And we were doing it wide out in the open, not caring who saw what.

I think about it, looking back. I believe Gwen thought herself above the rat race system society created, and she would not conform to it. Ever. The reason I could say this with an absolute is the wild look in her eyes; it was like her soul was being set free. At the same time, her smile was content, like when someone feels at peace in their life, true peace.

The kind of peace people with mountains of credit card debt, big house payments, and small cubicle jobs can never know.

Freedom.

Chapter 10

"Reasons, Reasons, Reasons,"

Dr. Remy had me meet with her in the small Feng Shui garden in the back of the facility at 9 a.m. sharp this Monday morning after she had me give her the tablet and keyboard at breakfast time. She had us sit in lawn chairs around the fire pit as the spring morning was cool, and Dr. Remy started a small fire for warmth.

"Good morning, Cliff," Dr. Remy said while sipping on her coffee and looking at what I had written.

"Good morning, ma'am," I said as I sat down before her.

"I liked how you used Hemingway's trope of the lady of dark," said Dr. Remy, "as Gwen's older sister being controlling, she was the lady of the dark, and the lady of the light trope being Gwen when she was most free. This is very good, because when we get into later chapters, you will begin to see who Gwen really is."

"I used to think Gwen was only dating me there for a while," I said openly, "that she was dating me in the beginning, as a middle finger to her sister. Gwen did give the poor woman the nickname, Mrs. Prude. Sorry, write on her addiction yet, as Gwen's sister's interference did play huge parts in our story."

Dr. Remy gave a slight chuckle before continuing.

"So you have given brief snapshots of your first meeting with Gwen," said Dr. Remy, "you met her friends according to previous writing. Did you ever meet her family on your first visit?"

"I met her Uncle and Aunt before flying back to the states," I said, "Her Uncle was a Navy Seal during Vietnam, and so he wanted to meet me, seeing I was a soldier."

"You said she had a tongue ring, Gwen's older than you, isn't she?" Dr. Remy asked

"Yeah, about ten years," I replied, "why does that matter?"

"Placing pieces together," She replied

I nodded my head softly.

"Does Gwen have other piercings?" Dr. Remy asked

"She got a piercing on her vagina when she found out I used to have my penis pierced," I told Dr. Remy, " I was dumb and 19, heard it made sex more intense for both parties. My body rejected the piercing, and I still had the scar. So, Gwen got her hoo-ha pierced, then her nipples after that. Gwen wanted to know the intense pleasure piercing could give a woman."

"That and impress the young,g vibrant man she was sleeping with," Dr. Remy said, as she leaned over and gave the tablet back.

"Gwen was barely 42 when you met her," Dr. Remy said as she leaned into her chair, "A single mom, with nothing to look forward to, and you were an anomaly she wasn't expecting."

"How did you know she was a mother?" I asked

"Her age," Dr. Remy replied, "Plus, my husband is Chinese, and we see it in modern western culture a lot. Asian men and women come from strict backgrounds that westerners don't come from, so certain people just rebel. They love their Asian heritage enjoy western freedoms and empowerments. It's a hard life to juggle, to figure out who you want to be when you're caught in two worlds at once."

"Which is why Gwen was so conservative at times and a madwoman at other times," I said

"Exactly," said Dr. Remy, "Do you have other dual identity friends or family?"

"Yeah," I replied, "in fact, I thought a few of them odd, or very hypocritical, to be honest. A friend got upset when her boyfriend admitted to watching porn and blamed men for being pigs, though a year prior, she ran an only fans account. I don't care what folks do in the life they want to live, but don't hate others for being themselves either."

"They're not hypocritical, they're just trying to find their own identity," Dr. Remy explained, "I always think about how hard this is for people of dual cultural identities, the movie Selena, when the father says, "We have to be more Mexican than the Mexicans, and more American than the American's." That's a hard life to have to walk as human beings by nature are deeply judgmental."

"When you put it that way… Walking on eggshells your whole life must be fuckin' brutal," I said.

"When with your culture, you act a certain way, eat certain foods," said Dr. Remy, "then you go to western culture, and people are way different. So you act one way at home, then a different way with your western friends. And in some cases when those two worlds meet, it is hard to appear in both Eastern and Western cultures."

Dr. Remy gave me a long pause for this new truth to sink within me.

"Do you give any thought as to why Gwen's sister was controlling?" asked Dr. Remy

"It is possible she been hurt by Gwen's addictive nature," I told her

"How so?" Dr. Remy asked

"The house Gwen lived in was bought for her by her sister," I said, "a good bit of time away from the city where Gwen's party friends were at. In fact, two houses were on the property so Gwen's younger sister could move on the property with her kids, as well. Gwen's older sister even got upset that Gwen never settled down with some rich rancher nearby."

"So, Gwen's older sister became a controller, due to Gwen's and possibly Gwen's younger sister, addictive and self-destructive behaviors," Dr. Remy said

"Yeah," I replied

"See, again, people who love addicts become controlling or manipulative," said Dr. Remy, "Lovers of addicts want to save the addict so badly, they do everything in their power to save the addict, even if that means becoming a supervillain of sorts. I doubt Gwen's older sister is a prude; I think she has done some crazy stuff in her life that only gets admitted at the family's drunk Christmas party. No one is perfect. The truth of addiction is it's a prison of the person's own making, so the key to their freedom has to come within the addict themselves. It's up to the addict to learn to love themselves properly and find a higher power to give their sobriety a purpose."

"I can give you that," I replied

"So, here's a heavier question," Dr. Remy asked, "why did the older sister want Gwen and the younger sister out of the "city life" so badly?"

"Because they lived dangerously for too long," I replied as therapy seemed to click

"Go on." Dr. Remy replied

"The younger sister was in a serious on and off-again relationship with a man who, from what Gwen told me, was the best friends with a gang leader of a gang that viewed the Hell's Angels as deadly enemies. The man had a severe drug issue where he would disappear on coke binges for long periods, then try to sober up and be a devout Muslim. Gwen's younger sister had two children with this man and wanted him in the kids' life," I told Dr. Remy

"And?" Dr. Remy asked

"Gwen's baby, daddy, was similar," I said, "But he grew up in a Christian home, became an atheist. Partied hard too, and Gwen had two children with him. The guy had many affairs and left Gwen multiple times."

"So why does your mind draw to the relationship of Gwen's sister this way?" Dr. Remy asked

"Because when Gwen broke things off with her ex and moved away," I said, "She began seeing this guy's brother as a friend with benefits, after what was described as a date rape on several occasions from Gwen, her sister, and this guy. They were doing coke, spiked the drinks on purpose, and Gwen ended up in this guy's brother's bed. To this day, this has me severely confused."

"Addiction is a monster," Dr. Remy replied, "it develops stock home syndrome with suppliers, and forgives egregious sins that the supplier does, to get the substance the addict needs. Again, you were an anomaly she wasn't expecting, Cliff. Plus, I doubt Gwen ever told her older sister any of this."

"She didn't," I replied, "Gwen thought her sister would see it as a person who brought this onto herself."

"Again, that's Gwen's addictive nature rationalizing not to get help," said Dr. Remy

"Can I ask you something doc'?" I asked

"Go ahead," Dr. Remy replied

"Why didn't you or your husband take on each other's last names?" I asked

"You are very observant," said Dr. Remy, "I have licenses and degrees in psychology and therapy, which is why some of our conversations are one or the other, sometimes, both. My husband has been a drug and alcohol counselor for 56 years. And during our time in this field, we learned humans need absolute freedom. So we live by that. A person taking a lover's name after marriage is an archaic symbol of ownership. Human beings should never be owned. No matter the opinion of a man's last name or a woman's last name, doing so shows ownership. "Humans are meant to be free, not possessions."

"How did you two come to this conclusion," I asked out of curiosity

"I'll explain it from your Christian view," Dr. Remy replied, "When God made man, and the first man named the first woman, they didn't use possessive naming. Nor anywhere in the Bible did this happen. When God named something or a person, it was either for: the potential of the person, place, or thing, a gift of God, or a miracle from God. Actions and obedience to God showed where a person belonged. The naming of a person as ownership comes from the sin of humankind, trying to be like God. Claiming the creation or ownership of something."

"You know that view is controversial as hell in world philosophy and most seminaries?" I asked rhetorically as a joke.

"Of course," replied Dr. Remy, "but I'm Hindu, and my husband studies Shinto. So, we don't care. And the reason why you joked rhetorically with me is you do believe in true Americanism. People of all colors, cultures, religions, and ideas can live harmoniously as one people."

I laughed a bit and nodded. Let Dr. Remy's words sink in, then she asked me another question, after analyzing me first—

"It's time to explore your view of God's providence," Dr. Remy said, "you are starting to see the parallels of your life. What did you see in your past that taught you to try to love Gwen, and why do you think God placed you in Gwen's life? Your Bible says in Ephesians 1:3-4 – God designs election and Predestination. Good and bad. You were destined to impact Gwen's life, and Gwen was destined to impact her life. Atheist philosophy calls this determinism, which I know you know, arguing that if we humans have free will, then Is God's predestination view a lie? How can someone have a future chosen for them before they existed and still have free will?

"You want me to explore this idea like The Matrix Revolutions movie tried to do?" I asked confused

"No," Dr. Remy replied," I think you were on a path to Gwen from your lifestyle from the Army, and you wanted to save someone from your past that you couldn't. Again, show me your friends, and I will show you your future. Your life story will help peel back the onion that is your trauma and why you gave up when you and Gwen fell apart. Why do you slowly kill yourself with drinking alone?"

"Ok, I know one layer of what you are saying, I admit to her, " but what is the other part, because now I'm confused?"

"Cliff," She said, " your blood work shows you drank dangerous levels daily. So I know you want to die. So I can, with an educated guess, see this program as one ditch of hope so you don't kill yourself. So you drink until you're completely sick. When you use the restroom, your gas and feces must smell like vomit. Which means, your stomach is on its way to shutting down or developing cancer or a severe ulcer. Blood work doesn't lie, Cliff."

She was right. Often I woke up hungover, or my bowel movements smelled like vomit. The only reason I checked into a clinic was I needed to know if my life had meaning. I needed to know why Gwen's leaving my life broke me so fuckin hard.

"So, what do I write next," I asked her

"This conversation, obviously," Dr. Remy replied, " and explore relations to Gwen's sister and yourself. The older one. The one you originally wrote in Hemingway's dark woman's trope. See where you two connect. View her not as an enemy, but someone is trying to save Gwen as you were trying, and why you two miscommunicated on deep levels."

"Fuck…, ok," I replied as I knew this was going to be hard.

"Before you go, tell me something you were raised to do, most find weird," Dr. Remy asked

"Pee outside," I told her, " growing up on horse ranches and Indian reservation land, I was taught that boys pee outside to save the water bill. Less water being flushed means less water being used."

"That's more common than you think," Dr. Remy laughed

"By the way," Dr. Remy said, " I am thinking that we should be meeting here for the next few weeks, I'll let you know. I want you to learn balance. It took eight men working in the hot sun, day in and day out, to construct this place for it to be a place of rest and a place of healing. Which will allow me to teach you about the hard work you're about to endure. So you too, can have a rest finally. Reason being, God rested on the 7th day, yet, you haven't. Not truly."

"Other words, to thine own self be true," I replied

"William Shakespeare, good" Dr. Remy replied, "Learn from Gwen's older sister, and from your worldview at the same time. See where you both are the same, and why you are both wildly different."

Just as I got up from my chair and gathered my things to leave, Dr. Remy stopped me in my tracks with a comment that still turns gears in my mind.

"You are a good man, Cliff," said Dr. Remy, "Gwen's world taught her that she was a play thing to be used. A woman with no meaning, or purpose. That her own life should just be enjoyed one party at a time, and that she was just someone to keep a man's bed warm. You with a heart of gold, tried reaching down to the sewers of humanity and save her from a nightmare. Your heart is too kind for you to crave death like you do. This dark world needs a light like you. You are far too good of a man to die in a shit hole, alone."

This next chapter is going to be rough. I knew what Dr. Remy meant by that last comment, and though my soul was tired, I knew I needed to learn what God and Dr. Remy both were teaching me.

Chapter 11

"Rebellion, a Healthy Dose of It."

*D*oc' this is not in relation to your assignment, or maybe it is. When I see you Wednesday, we'll talk.

Recently before rehab, I reconnected with my English teacher, who taught me about life and the truth of literature. Like, the reason books have been so important for so long is they are the birth of everything else. Books were written to tell the world what stories existed, and poetry came from the summation of those stories to tell the truth of the human soul interacting with life itself. My English teacher often quoted this to his prized students and the students who reached out to him, "Remember, the aim of life is to be real, not perfect. We are a whisp soul, hauling a corpse." Which was a play on words of the famous words by Epictetus. The romantic bastard gave up teaching and now farms in Idaho.

Because of him (my English teacher), I fell in love with literature. I even watched my first romantic movie, "Dead Poets Society." A film of young boys trying to learn life, and here is this radical teacher, jumping on desks and quoting Shakespeare. Teaching these poor lost boys the meaning of life by saying, "Medicine, law, business, engineering, these are all noble pursuits, and necessary to sustain life. But poetry, beauty, romance, love, these are what we stay alive for."

My English teacher always would remind us his favorite line in the film to keep us, students, from being overtly stupid and brash is, "there is a time for daring, and there is a time for caution. And a wise man understands which is called for." Of course, this comes from a man who wore ancient battle armor to school to educate poor town students in ancient poems and literature, while small-minded folks freaked out. No, seriously, the guy dressed as a knight one day, so we could understand what Chaucer, Dumas, and Shakespeare were talking about with visual reference.

But my favorite memory of this English teacher wasn't when we talked about "Dante's Inferno," but when he challenged us to taste the rain. It was raining during the last period, and he was trying to teach us about life between the realist and the romantic writer. So, My English Teacher swung the door open, and invited all of us students to go outside with him in the rain.

I followed my teacher as I wanted to learn. Some students came out with us to feel the rain; others didn't. Then my English teacher showed me the true meaning of romance that day when he said, "Those of us now, feeling the water on our skin. Tasting the cold weather on our lips are romantics. We live for the experience, the passion of life. Those in the classroom are the realists. They know many of us will work hard jobs that will curse the rain. No one is ever right or wrong. Life is an experience from your perspective and no one else's. Who you are is the existence you desire to experience. Some will become bankers, hate it, and fall in love with swinging hammers. Some of us will desire to be preachers in our own faith or philosophy, and God themself will tell you to sit down and shut up. The point is, who you are, is what you want to be. What you accept, what you settle for, or what you rise against, defines your mortal legacy."

So here is me being real instead of perfect and sharing a piece of me before going deeply into Gwen's sister's background.

I used to think myself so suave and debonair when I would quote James O' Barr's "The Crow," "It doesn't rain all the time," which was from The Crow movie and not the actual book. Jane Siberry came up with the song, and for some reason, its main poetic line stuck and was repeated in the movie several times.

In the book, James O'Barr was inspired to create the story through the real-life turmoil of his love dying and, in his grief, read an article about gang violence. So, armed with his artistic ability and a slew of new wave and punk music records, James O'barr created "The Crow." A hero comes back from the dead to avenge the murder of his beloved. And yes, I admit, if it weren't for The Crow, I would have never heard of or appreciated musical acts like "New World Order" or "Joy Division." The book acts as a love letter to the writings of Joy Division's lead singer and the new lead singer who took over for the band after his suicide and created New World Order. The Crow was James O'Barr venting out love lost.

In real life, James O'Barr created The Crow when he was grieving the loss of his girlfriend as she passed away. James was reading a newspaper at the time and saw two lovers had been gunned down in some city, and in his grief, allowed that tragic story to help inspire him to create a gothic superhero in the vein of "The Count of Monte Cristo."

However, my true story, in fourth grade? Matthew (my best friend since fourth grade) often stole this comic book or "graphic novel" from Matthew's older brother's room and read it. We knew it was cool or good writing when the hero killed a drug pusher in it and wrote, "I KNOW WHY JESUS DIED MOTHER FUCKER", right behind the bad guy in blood. Because only good writing curses, right? Ah, we were dumb kids; what can I say? At that age, curse words were so "cool" in movies and books.

As life went on, I explored that book more and more. Until I found myself romantic, loving books like "The Count of Monte Cristo" and "TheThree Musketeers." What can I say, Alexander Dumas was a prolific writer.

In "Count" he writes of love lost through dubious means, and in "Musketeers" novel series, he writes of many loves that cannot be due to poor people loving rich people or honor and duty overtaking the purpose of love. But love nonetheless was his main focus. And I have been criminal to everything Mr.Dumas had written.

I focused so intensely on my military occupation that I never questioned what it did to my love life until my personal morals and worldview came into my mind and started asking questions, "why?" When I lost a lover or two, I admit my selfish pride was my call to duty and honor.

I even tried loving a wealthy girl once, in my early 20's. I understand now why Dumas wrote D'Artagnan, always having unacquainted love. It's hard for people of different social structures to be at each other's eye level. The poor are always working hard to prove themselves, and yet, never enough for the rich. Though the sex was great for a 21-year-olds standard, it was nothing to build something life-affirming.

Though I never took revenge on someone for love, I understand why men and women alike would burn the world down for love.

There is so much about Gwen I long for, and yet, I admit, I really do not understand. It's an odd ball of confusion and longing.

Also, working on this project, I noticed something interesting. Worlds collide at the same time as I write my words. People need to use the phone in the recreation room and speak loudly, almost screaming in the phone at a loved one, so no one else can do or want to do anything else they wish to do. Or people need to make right by a loved one and need to cook for family coming for a visit, and so, I stop writing and help. This therapy teaches me to understand human beings on a compassionate level again. See worldviews outside my anger and hopelessness.

Funny, as I write this, I am listening to Dean Lewis, "Be Alright." An outlaw country from the new generation of songwriters.

When I was a kid, I was told by most people growing up, don't listen to country music; it's horrible. Listen to rap or rock, or this or that. So growing up, I hated country music with a passion. Thinking it was a lesser art form. Yet, I grew up on horse ranches and Navajo tribal lands. Country Music communicated between my dad and me and how my grandfather taught me about life.

Thinking about it now, my rebellious soul came from them and why I connected with Gwen. Here's why. My dad was a mild-mannered man when I was growing up, yet, he had a wild streak a country mile wide in his youth.

My whole life, I thought he was just a hard-working mechanic who never really broke the rules. Yet, as I got older working in diners in my hometown, I learned of his small-town myths. My dad was a bad boy. The kind women whispered about, and old men wished they were.

My dad had a muscle car he would only drive when he wanted to drag race, and our small-town cops would escort him home when that car came out of the garage. And another story of him as he raced motorcycles backward on the town dirt track. The same dirt track Steve McQueen the movie star raced on here in southern California (seriously, google Menifee or Perris California). I guess my dad started a popular event in his youth.

Riders got on dirt motorcycles and sat backwards and tried to ride the damn things in a different way. My dad won most nights that way. However, this failed in comparison to the small-town hero story of my dad, that even his mother, my grandmother, attested to.

My dad broke his leg horseback riding one weekend, and in order to race his motorcycle that coming weekend, he painted his leg cast black and put on a motorcycle riding boot to hide it. Why did he do this? To earn the love and respect of my mother in a dramatic fashion.

Engines revved up, and the whole town was watching. My dad put it on the line and raced as fast as he could through the pain in his body was ungodly. But why would this small-town boy do this?

My real dad was a bastard. A monster in the closet. A man who beat his wife and kids, and one night my mom ran to her dad from Arizona to California. The reason she fled from the monster is cause the fucker broke her cheekbone and snapped my brother's arm like a twig for covering my body for getting a beating at just nine months old.

And my bad boy stepdad stepped up, like a badass out of Hollywood western films, to save a damsel in distress and make all's right with the world. My dad took my mom and us kids to the race track when they were dating every Friday night. Bought her flowers. He made dates where he would rent movies on the weekends, and pizza, so my mom could see new films and have an adult friend without leaving the kids behind.

My real dad was trying to get my mom back by coming into town every forte night, even after she met and fell in love with my stepdad. Now I don't know how my stepdad broke his leg, nor have I ever asked. All I know is my stepdad, my father, claimed my mother and me in a badass moment from a monster in glorious fashion. In a way, that said, "Fuck you, and the goddamn horse you road in. This is my family."

Is this story true? I don't know. Maybe a small-town legend meets the truth on this one like a three-dollar bill existing. But, people where I come from loving the lore. And yeah, they over embellish it a bit at times. Though I can say this. My grandmother, over the mantle of her fireplace, has a photo of my father with a devilish grin standing over the monster. The monster has a wicked broken nose and is being handcuffed by two cops as if the cops did not care that his nose had been eradicated. Grandma makes damn sure I see it when I visit her too. A trophy of honor grandma calls it, So something happened that night. I can't tell you the truth because I don't know.

All I know is George is my dad, and that is that. My "Real Dad" can eat it. George stepped up and was the hero of me. So I'll take a small town b.s. over public opinion, any day. The public told me, "what's cool" "what you should do," and my dad didn't give a damn; he made his own rules. In the end, my mother and my family were my father's choices. He was a man's man.

Which is why I still believe in the American rebel: the cowboy, the outlaw, the person who fights to make things right. The person who straps up and does what is hard, good people deserve good things.

So I understand the wildfire of the soul. I do. But why does it consume us and ruin others' moments, hours, or other lives in the process? What am I missing, I wonder?"

My grandfather was a good lesson in life, to know your limits.

My grandfather was a cowboy outlaw that made his own damn luck. So by being himself, Grandpa became a millionaire. How did my grandfather do this? By building a successful general contracting business.

Grandpa was smart. First, he started as a lawn maintenance person; then, when he saved up enough money, he bought the tools to do landscaping. And then, grandpa would save his money from job sites and buy extensive construction equipment like tractors, haulers, and pneumatic power tools.

The lawn maintenance and tree trimming side of the business was to help keep workers busy in the slow months, and Grandpa even got the brilliant idea to rent his tractor equipment out to other contractors. Grandpa first would get the tractor rental prices of the big chain stores and made sure his tractors were 30% cheaper to rent. So, yeah, Grandpa took some loss on the rentals, but for a purpose.

Grandpa's business loaded, transported, and delivered all the equipment he rented out, so Grandpa's business was on every job site. Basically, advertising to the more prominent contract builders to do business with Grandpa. The tractor rental made Grandpa look bigger than what he actually was. And big chain stores do not want to really work with small construction businesses; they prefer big established companies. So Grandpa taught me when it comes to business, if you look big and important, you'll be big and important.

Grandpa also taught me to spend the money you don't own so you can save yours. Grandpa knew every builder and land tycoon were taking huge loans from banks to develop shopping malls and houses. So, since Grandpa usually got the big contract deals with chain stores everyone wanted, these people pulling the loans wanted those chain stores in their development deals. And for a small 3% fee of the loan they took out, Grandpa would be a good reference for the builder. And with Grandpa's name already attached, the chain stores trusted it was an excellent development to be a part of.

So, Grandpa saved his own money and only spent his "gift money" for helping folks get bank loans. Everything was going good for him. Until one day, the money made Grandpa feel like a god. And that's the day my Dad didn't allow us to see Grandpa anymore.

Grandpa eventually got into a bad woman, gambling, and then drugs. And he was not just using drugs either, selling them. Grandpa even used his own business to transport them.

Grandpa got busted when I was 16, lost everything, and went to prison for eight long years. How My Grandfather still owns a ten-acre horse ranch, I don't know. But I see the tax man loves giving him hassles every tax season. Grandpa has learned his lesson, though, became a good man again and watches over my grandmother and a few others.

All the while, Grandpa had a wild hair up his ass that turned his brain to kitchen soup; Grandma fought for his soul. And in the end, Grandma won. Grandma did not chase Grandpa around town or cry her eyes out when he was a dog. Grandma remained a lady and prayed for him at church every mass.

Grandma never slandered Grandpa's name, never allowed folks who would talk ill of him in her house. Nor did she ever listen to the town's gossip as she kept herself respectful and did what all ladies do. Take care of the grandbabies, and make sure the grandbabies never see their hero acting like a supervillain. Grandpa struck gold with Grandma; now I think about it. Pure gold.

It also taught me a valuable lesson, which is why I never chased Gwen. People only change for the one they deem worth it. And a person who wants to be in your life will choose to be in it. So though I love Gwen from a great distance, it is possible I'm not the holy one that her heart dreams of.

I admit I do the same for Gwen, as Grandma did for Grandpa. I pray Gwen gets the perfect life, a life worth living. And that Gwen finds the true love of her life that makes every morning feel like a child on Christmas morning.

There are many nights like this one where I miss Gwen as if my soul knows she's the missing piece. Where I want to, taste the fire in her kiss. See the storm of her soul rage in her eyes. Let her beauty leave me speechless as my tongue lay limp in my mouth. As I breathed in her every last breath as if it was the only thing keeping me alive.

And then hear her whisper, "Everything will be ok."

My heart begs for one moment, just one last time like this. But my brain knows if my heart ever got it, I wouldn't be able to let her go. Because in those divine moments of her bed, no one else existed. It was just us. It's like my soul knows Gwen is home and is constantly screaming to go back, ever since.

Here is the snippet of the song I listen to when I think about Gwen.

"We ain't never been good at being long-distance lovers

I guess it is what it is

And that's the heartbreak I still can't forget

Cause she was the right girl

Yes, she was all mine

Thought about her all-day

We spent every night

Chasing down the stars

Talking 'bout forever

But I learned the hard way

Never say never

It's too bad that clocks can't stop on a dime...

Cause she was the right girl

The right girl at the wrong time."

— Jon Langston
"Right Girl, Wrong Time"

Chapter 12

"Understanding Hatred"

I never knew what it was like to be hated for just existing before. I found it very weird. I never met Gwen's older sister before she found out we were dating, and I did not meet her before she found the dreaded "pantie photo" on Gwen's phone. I kind of understood, but not really; the photo wasn't real lewd or showed Gwen's face. Yet, I admit, there is the distinct possibility that Gwen didn't tell me the whole story. However, to this day, Gwen's older sister always seemed a bit "off."

For this story, I will name Gwen's older sister, Vickie. This way, no one can know who I am talking about or feel like I am bad-mouthing someone behind their back. Most couldn't connect the dots that Gwen and Vickie are sisters anyway, not unless they shared their family history with you. Both Gwen and Vickie drastically changed their real names for more western names, and they didn't choose similar names.

I later learned the reason why some Asian cultures did this growing up in the '80s and early '90s was to fit in more so they wouldn't be shamed by westerners for being too weird. When Gwen explained that her friends and family lived by western names to fit in so they wouldn't get picked on, or so Westerners could say their names correctly, it just felt wrong. Like why should a person have to change themselves so much just to fit in Australia or America?

Girls would choose more western names. Some girls, when coming to more western countries, would choose movie star names like Angelina Jolie or Julia Roberts, the rationale for this, since Julia and Angelina were famous names, they would be easy to recognize and pronounce. I didn't find this out until my neighbor Tran told me why his wife went by Jamie as in Jamie Lee Curtis, instead of her real name, Yo-yo.

The more I write this, the more Gwen's past seems harsh and her sister more understandable. In today's society, at least here in America, Asian names are more accepted. At least in the areas where I am from in San Diego and San Diego county. The culture shift of just being yourself is coming more into acceptance than past generations. Though I still see some Asian girls go by more western names than the name their family gave them at birth.

So, who was Vickie? Someone who I see from my perspective as 50% real and 50% fake as hell. Gwen told me that her sister was "famous" and nervous about me meeting Vickie. So, when the photo was found out on Gwen's phone, Gwen finally told me who her sister was.

"My sister thinks you might be using me," said Gwen, "to tarnish her reputation."

Which is why I think Vickie is 50% fake. The first thought out of Vickie's mind was how someone could use her family to hurt her own "celebrity" status, then worry about her actual family first, which I found weird.

But then again, I have always viewed "fame" as a poor person's drug. I'll share what I mean at the end of this Vickie thing.

So, I finally had to find out who Vickie thought she was. Without trying to sound mean, there are famous people, and there are famous people in their own social group or niche.

For instance, if I said the name Brad Pitt or Tom Cruise, like them, hate them, or seen a movie they made or not, everyone on the planet knows who they are. No matter where they go, Mr. Pitt and Mr. Cruise will have millions of obsessed fans tracking them down wherever they go. Why? Because they, for some reason, have the "it" factor that makes them excel in their field of work, unlike many others. No one knows what that "it" factor is. Just some people got it, and some don't. But because of "it," some people transcend to god-like fame, and everything they touch turns to gold.

Then some famous people are recognized in your circle or niche, like the 12-year-old kid getting famous for playing video games and uploading his videos to YouTube. To the people within the community of youtube and gaming, this 12-year-old kid is a rock star. But for people like me who don't care for youtube or video games, we will not know or care to know who this 12-year-old kid is.

Then there is a person only famous in their country, state or province, or city. Whatever the person does impacts only their people or the people they represent. For instance, hardly anyone outside of America knows Kevin Smith, the director. But if you are a part of the cult of Kevin Smith, you'll know who I am talking about. You will know of Kevin Smith by his comedy specials, podcast, and the films he writes and directs. And if you are not into stoner comedies that make fun of social constructs like organized religion like Smith's "Dogma" does, you're not going to care.

Knowing of Kevin Smith is like you saying, "I like Rocky road ice cream the best."

and I say in return, "I don't like ice cream; I prefer gelato."

Though I will say this, Kevin Smith has the best boss movie in Indy film-making history. People protested against his film "Dogma," and he showed up to the protest to protest his own movie. So when the news stations covered it, people saw how silly this protest against his film was, and gained more national attention than what the protesters wanted.

Vickie wrote a memoir on surviving the Vietnam war and escaping to Australia. The book sold well on Amazon and received Amazon's international bestsellers award, a year before the journalist exposed what a scam that award was with his book, "My Left Foot." Seriously, Vickie's book came out in 2014, and this journalist, four months later in 2015, exposed why people shouldn't trust the Amazon rating system that Vickie's book got. No fault of Vickie, but it made people less trusting of the Amazon bestseller label for a while.

The reporter uploaded a blank manuscript, took a picture of his left foot, and used it as the cover image for his "book." Then showed how he earned an Amazon best-selling badge on the book by knowing how the Amazon tracking system worked. Which is why starting in 2016, there weren't any major news outlets covering Amazon Best Sellers anymore, only New York Bestsellers and old sales tracking systems for new best authors.

The reporter who wrote this article gave Amazon a black eye and possibly hurt new and upcoming authors who can't afford to go through the traditional publication system.

But, this was late 2014 and early 2015. Sydney news outlets and radio stations were covering Vickie's book and interviewing her about it. I believe Vickie made it in the sweet moment of fame, at the right place, at the right time. Which for anyone to do, is a feat within itself. Having your stars align to where you gain success and notoriety in any niche of the social consciousness is a mere act of God smiling favorably on you. So, Vickie's accomplishment should not be taken lightly.

Where it gets ugly for me is as Gwen dated and traveled to see each other every other month when we could, Vickie would send footage of war crimes that U.S. soldiers did in Afghanistan, saying, "If he is a good man, how come his people did this?"

As for me to answer for other evil men's actions. Not once did I make Vickie answer for the gang life that happened in Cabramatta that exploded in the late 80s and early 90s, where Vietnamese gang members called 5T gunned down whole families.

I was as unrelated to the war criminals as Vickie was to the gang members. Asking someone to answer for crimes they were not a part of is unjust. If society thought that way, society would have fewer people because we are all somehow, shape, or form related to an individual who has committed a violent crime. Our justice systems would be unsustainable.

But here I was, according to Vickie, responsible for a horrific act, that the criminals were caught, imprisoned, or sent to the death penalty for breaking rules of war set by the United Nations. As I said, I find Vickie's natural hate for me very weird.

I tried to reason with it as Americans were the popular force in Vietnam during the Vietnam war, even though there were both French forces, British forces, and Australian forces in the war. And within that war itself, no one can tell you the real reasons why America really got involved by siding with the French soldiers who the communists attacked. Every history book, documentary, and article covering the Vietnam war tells the most convoluted story.

But, I wasn't born yet, nor was I conceived. I know that The Vietnam war is a bitter story in history no one likes talking about. That its origins and reasons change from country to country.

Thanks to my world travel, I know the French tell a different reason for the war than the one I grew up with in America. And the U.K.'s story of the war contradicts both France's and America's versions. And Australia's view on it contradicted all the accounts of France, the USA, and the U.K. It's like the "free world" knew it royally fucked up and blamed everyone else.

It is popular to hate the Vietnam war, but no country that was involved in the damn thing can tell you exactly why we fought it or why we fought it in the first place if every nation involved in it was against it.

Living as a war veteran, the only thing I can say is this. War is the most inhumane way of communicating a religious, political, or social-economic view that humankind has ever invented. It is where monsters are created, and innocence is hurt. I once saw a Taliban soldier use a child as a human meat shield as he shot at me. All I could remember was the fear in that poor kid's eyes, praying I wouldn't shoot back, so I never did. I just hid behind a rock and let the Taliban soldier run out of bullets. Then, when he was empty, I arrested him and took him to the Afghan Army to serve justice.

Then when I got back to the states, I met and became dear friends with an Afghan woman who thanked me for fighting for the freedom of their country. Moving on cause this talk is giving fuckin anxiety.

Part 2 of this. Sorry, my last entry triggered old memories, and I had to take a day away from this, Doc'.

After Gwen's and mine's Hawaii moment, and we were planning to get Gwen off government aid and live together, Vickie put the house she bought Gwen in Gwen's name only. Sighting-

"You don't know my sister's history," Vickie told me, eye to eye, " I don't want to get sued by you if you get hurt on the property if you both decide to live here in Australia or have the house being sold for possible illegal activity if you two decide to move to America."

As I said, Vickie was brutal to me.

This is funny because technically, Gwen and Vickie both broke the law twice concerning Gwen's house. Gwen almost got back with her baby daddy, so he had stuff being mailed to her house, and they even went on vacation in Vietnam together when He tried getting Gwen back.

Neither Vickie nor Gwen reported this to the government. On paper, it looked as if they lived together, and Vickie knew about it, and supported it. Meaning they defrauded the Australian government thousands of dollars.

And after that fling ran its course, Gwen let her new boyfriend before me move in. And again, no one reported to the government that Gwen had a partner helping her or living with her that was very well off to the point he made 500k a year.

Now, I personally don't care what people do if it has nothing to do with me. But being accused by someone saying I might break the law after they clearly broke the law, I find hypocritically funny.

There for a while after Gwen was rushed to the hospital for a sickness that almost severely hurt her, to where I had to reach out to Vickie. I didn't care if Vickie hated my guts, Gwen was her sister, and family needed to be there when bad stuff was happening.

After this incident Vickie texted us both, Gwen and I, in a group chat what seemed to be a heartfelt apology. Things seemed good for a brief while, but when Gwen and I had our very public break up, Vickie's claws came back out.

I won't share the vindictive crap Vickie texted me the next few days after, but it was clear her "friendship" with me after Gwen's hospital visit wasn't sincere.

All I can think of why Vickie hated me so much was I was American, I was a soldier, and Gwen sent me naked photos. I was the unholy trinity of what Vickie did not want for her sister. The Vietnam war was cruel. Though I had nothing to do with that war, I represent a nation that fought in it.But again, Vickie was punishing me for something I had no part in.

The only reason I believe Vickie was not genuine with her story was after seeing this new article on different news stations; I googled Vickie again and read interviews she gave in the course of the time her book was popular. And what I saw was substantial hypocritical differences in things she said at different times to different news sources, which, unfortunately for Vickie, is starting to be pointed out in the court of public opinion.

That and at dinner conversations Vickie told these heroic tales of her and her parents journey on a refugee boat, that later Gwen and Vickie's Uncle proved to me were a lie. Their Uncle became a Navy Seal for the American's and when the soldier's left Vietnam, Vickie was claimed as her

Uncle's daughter, and was flown out of Vietnam on an American plane to an joint operating Australian-American Air Base in Northern Territory known as Pine Gap. Pine Gap was a military base in the 60s and 70s. Sometime in the 80s, Pine Gap got turned into a surveillance base for spies and diplomats.

From there the Uncle moved her to Sydney and enrolled her into private schools. Vickie then went to college, learned real estate, and became rich. Which is why the Uncle hates Vickie's book so much. The Uncle joined the American forces os that he and his family could leave Vietnam for a better country within the free world, as Vietnam at the time, was torn by war and under developed by poverty. The Uncle feels betrayed by Vickie as he almost died trying to give her a better chance at life and Vickie lives this lie.

Now Vickie's and Gwen's parents were refugees, and got placed in the Australian camps. Which when I talked to the people who had to go through all that, my heart broke. That sounds horrible. Gwen and Vickie's dad didn't want to fight in the war, so he refused to choose any side. But as the war got worse, Gwen's dad asked the Uncle to take Vickie with him to Australia.

According to Gwen's dad, and uncle, Vickie would have been one years old when Vickie was flown out of Vietnam with her uncle in 1972. A full year before western forces got out of Vietnam. Not only that the father said the region they were living in had been untouched by the war, but when the dad found out America was leaving in the following year, and knew his brother was leaving in a weeks time to go to Australia with his family; Vickie's father gave her to his brother who claimed her as his own on paperwork.

And my genuine fear for Vickie, because honestly, I feel she is probably a sweet and loving person to those she cares for if she does try to write a sequel book to her success? The way "cancel culture" is, and how people these days are ready to crucify other people for stuff they did decades ago, there might be a smart-ass reporter knowing of these contradictions and will ambush Vickie during an interview. And people in a mob-like frenzy go after her. I honestly pray Vickie rises above it gloriously if it does happen to her.

The reason I share this, I view cancel culture as brutally unjust at times, and people take it wildly too far. Sometimes it feels as if a considerable part of cancel culture scours the internet for reasons to hate people doing better than them, and find a reason to burn a person's reputation to the ground so they can no longer be successful because the person doing the "Canceling," is unhappy with their own life and desires the world to burn.

Lastly, about Vickie's texts before Hawaii. Vickie believes in "The Secret" and other related religious views of the power of speaking things into existence. Reading Vickie's texts (which confuses me), why would a person text a loved one you were trying to save, and tell them horrible things were on their way to them? It was as if Vickie was trying to conjure bad things to happen because Gwen wasn't listening to her. I get it it's there spiritual belief, but it's confusing. Why curse a person you love and wish bad things on them?

I don't share this belief to be honest, of power in the tongue. But still. If you truly believed your words have the power, why would you confess a horrible thing over someone you loved? The more, and more, I write about Vickie, the more and more she contradicts herself in words and actions, which deeply confuses me. I do not love or hate Vickie, just wildly confused as to who or what she is.

Even as I wrote this, one of the people I have come to know came into the day room to watch the new version of Westside Story with her grandmother. So I took a break, and watched it with them. The scenes were wildly changed from the original, but the music stayed the same. But it did shed some light in my heart in how I can try to understand Vickie more.

I know I have written unflattering things of Vickie, which is why I changed her name in this therapy writing to protect her. Especially after watching Westside Story again, I feel I need to protect her even more.

In Westside Story, it's a musical retelling of Romeo and Juliet. However, the story takes place in Westside New York, between two rival street gangs known as the Jets and the Sharks. Tony the lead romantic male in the film, belongs to the Jets. An Maria the romantic female lead, her brother leads The Sharks.

In the film when violence happened and some one got hurt or murdered, the fully story was never told. Each side would only tell how vile the other side was, and never admit their side vile actions. It was like each side wanted to be heroes, and never the villains. When in fact, both sides were evil.

Tony many times tried to stop the fights and be an honorable man. But, in the end, Maria loses her bother and Tony to gang violence. And it is only when three people lay dead from the violence, the gangs stop fighting.

Just like an allegory for war. No side ever tells the truth and wants to be viewed as the heroes. And the violence finally stops when enough people are tired of mourning the dead.

In this film is where I begin to understand Vickie. Maria's older brother Bernardo, doesn't want Maria to date an American. And in the end, Bernardo ends up hurting Maria deeply by dying in a knife fight over this belief.

What is even more interesting is interesting is Bernardo wanted the best for Maria and tried to get her to date a boy who was well educated and going to college. But when the college boy decides to partake in the gang violence, Bernardo half heartedly tells the college boy no. But still allows the college boy to join the gang fight.

Just like how Vickie was ok with Gwen seeing other men who were Australian, and or Vietnamese. And how Vickie even tried to get Gwen to date someone of Vickie's approval. I deeply understand Vickie loves her sister and wants to do anything to save her sisters life from the life Gwen had been living. And it is with this understanding I can forgive Vickie for being cruel to me.

Sure, Vickie has her own sins that has caused a rift between herself and her Uncle, and Father. But that is between them. As for me, I can forgive because I can see a sister bending over backwards to save her sister from living a constant nightmare.

We all have our own sinful cross to carry. Vickie, like I, was fighting for the life and love of Gwen. I can't fault her for that.

Chapter 13

"Wednesday Aftermath"

The therapy appointment was at two o'clock today, and we met in the staff kitchen area instead of the Garden. I saw Dr. Remy cutting fresh vegetables to make a veggie meal of some sort.

"Sit on the stool next to the counter," Dr. Remy advised me, "don't worry about giving me the tablet here on out; I just found out I can check your progress on my work phone and computer. And yes, I saw how hard the last "chapter" was to write for you. Your day-long break shared some insights."

"So what now?" I asked

"Why didn't you tell me about your daughter's death?" asked Dr. Remy, "that is a huge piece of information not to share with me, which means you don't trust me."

"It's not something I like to talk about," I said sternly, though I know Dr. Remy could feel the anger in my voice.

"As I said, trauma is a layered onion," Dr. Remy said, as she continued to chop away various vegetables, "galaxy, play country music, 90's."

And just like that, Dr. Remy's smartphone started playing country music.

"Why are you playing country?" I asked

"You grew up with it, and it brings you comfort in uncomfortable times," said Dr. Remy, "in your last journal entry, you admitted to listening to country music just right before writing about "Vickie." Which the relation to Vickie upsets you, and you leaned on childhood memory to keep you calm."

"I still feel like I talked shit on that woman," I said

"Leave your guilt at the door, Cliff," Dr. Remy said, "I have been a clinician for rehab therapy for a long time. You used a fake name for Gwen's sister, and you never share Gwen's real name or even give Gwen or her sister last names in your story entries, for a lovely reason."

"What purpose is that, doc'?" I retorted in a low tone. I admit I was getting angry at the thought of Dr. Remy knowing of my daughter's passing.

"Honor and protection," Dr. Remy said calmly as she began to mix the veggies in a salad bowl, "which means you are willing to explore your past and get better, but not at the risk of exposing others' sins."

"That, and what my grandfather told me once," I replied.

"Which is?" Dr. Remy asked

"Truth is a four-sided room," I told her, "There is what I said happened. There will be what the person I had the issue with will say that happened. There will be people listening to both sides of the story or just one side of the story and drawing their conclusions of what happened. And the fourth wall of the room is what actually happened, which is hardly ever seen."

"See, a great listener, Cliff," Dr. Remy said as she served us both a chef salad.

While we ate a few bites of food, Dr. Remy gave space for us to let the tension cool before talking again.

"You want to know what I like about the story of Jesus?" Dr. Remy said

"No," I replied

"In times Jesus was teaching uncomfortable truths, truths that would upset folks," Dr. Remy said, "Jesus talked it over with a meal, to keep people calm, and in a communal mindset."

"Which is why we are meeting here today, over food and country music," I said

"Gwen didn't show up for your daughter's funeral, did she?" Dr. Remy asked

"No, she didn't," I told her.

I could feel my anger deepening in my soul, which made me not want to eat anymore.

"What happened?"

"Gwen went out partying the night before her flight," I said, as I began playing with my food, "she was supposed to fly out that morning but missed it cause she went out hardcore binge partying with her "friends." Gwen was dropped off at her Uncle's with powder on her nose and completely incoherent. The doctors found coke, loads of alcohol, madma, and muscle relaxers in her system.

"And so the ignition switch was lit to burn your relationship with Gwen to the ground," Dr. Remy said.

Again, she allowed a good pause for me to cry it out some and breathe to get a handle on my emotions.

"Cliff, I want you to understand something," Dr. Remy said, as she wiped salad dressing from her lower lip, "You loved Gwen with a love most women pray for from whatever God they ask. You fought hard for her heart and gave her the best of you. The way you write about her, even in the intimate details, shows absolute reference with complete ardent worship. No one would read your words as smut or trash, but a man caught in the whims of a woman he tried to love. Also, you are still not seeing Gwen's viewpoint."

As I began to settle down and grab my composer the best I could as Dr. Remy set her food aside and grabbed a cup of sugar, with a cup of sweetener and another cup with salt, and placed them right in front of me. Then, Dr. Remy grabbed a giant-sized mug and put it right before the other three mugs.

Dr. Remy pointed to the empty mug and said, "This is Gwen, and she is empty and thirsty for sugar."

Dr. Remy then began to pour the entire cup of sugar into the mug.

"You loved Gwen and poured yourself onto her altar," Dr. Remy said as the sugar cup emptied, "but Gwen needed more than you could give, so you gave her something sweet, but it wasn't sugar."

Then Dr. Remy started pouring the sweetener into the mug until the sweetener cup was completely empty,

"Lastly, you had no more sugar and sweetness to give," Dr. Remy said, "so you gave her what was bitter inside you because you were spent."

Dr. Remy then poured the entire salt cup into the mug.

"The problem with addiction," Dr. Remy said, "It's an empty giant mug that needs to be filled, so loved ones try to fill it one way or another. But the truth is only the addict can figure out what they are missing. And so when a loved one poured everything they had into the addict, what happens?"

"What?" I asked

Dr. Remy then took the filled mug of sugar, sweetener, and salt, and dropped it to the ground, and let it break into a thousand pieces, making a giant mess on the floor.

"They destroy themselves, and everything you pour into them," said Dr. Remy, "addiction is a demon like no other. Because I promise you, Gwen probably analyzed you and missed you like crazy when you two were done. Gwen, like you, was living in hell."

"There for a bit, for a few months after things ended," I told Dr. Remy, "I would get private number calls; I knew it was her. Because when I picked up, I knew it was her breathing on the other side of the phone. She wouldn't say anything, nor would I, and she would just hang up."

"See?" said Dr. Remy

"So what do I do doc'?" I asked

"You're doing it, you're healing," Dr. Remy said, "Now to cover why you never share about your daughter's death with anyone."

"Do I have to share that now?" I asked timidly, I admit, as I didn't want to.

"No, we're not there yet," Dr. Remy said, "we need to deal with all of Gwen's past sins that snowballed like a powder keg, so when she didn't show up to your daughter's funeral, it exploded and burned the love you tried to give her to the ground. As I said, the love you gave Gwen is the love of legends. What was your daughter's name?"

"Sam," I said

"Short for Samantha," Dr. Remy said

"yeah," I said, "and sometimes I would call her Samie."

At this point, my rage was setting in too deep, and I needed something positive.

"A father's nickname for a child is always the true name," Dr. Remy said.

Again she gave me time to cool down as she swept up the mess she created by dropping the mug on the floor. As she did, I finished my dinner.

"Why did you have me write about my romantic encounters with Gwen?" I asked

"Two reasons, one reason, you're not ready yet, to hear," Dr. Remy, "the other reason is, I need you to remember who Gwen is. The good loving mother, lover, and friend she truly was to you. And her lady of the dark, her addiction, is what destroyed you two. This way, you can forgive her and yourself, so we can address the other major two parts that drove you to give up on life."

"Meaning?" I asked

"You saw your grandfather suffer for his crimes," Dr. Remy said, "and come out a better man. You hear stories of your bad boy dad fighting for his family in your hometown. Your worldview is very black and white. Good guys win; bad guys lose. People are more complicated than that. Always have been."

"And?" I asked, being somewhat smug cause I just didn't want to talk anymore.

"You forgot something in your self-righteous personal exile into hell," Dr. Remy replied

"Which?" I asked because this one comment she made; this sentence grabbed my attention like no other

"Grace," Dr. Remy said.

Again Dr. Remy, in her wisdom, paused and let the word sink into my brain like a sack of hammers breaking my pride.

"Do you know the story in the book of the Bible, 2 Kings 5:1-27?" asked Dr. Remy

"Yes," I said

"Tell it to me in short term form," Dr. Remy said

"A general who led armies against God's people," I told her, "hid the fact he had leprosy from his people, as they would've outcast him. The general's servant girl, who was enslaved and a trophy of war, advised him to see the prophet of God, and so he did. The general gets healed and promises to follow God, and hopes God will forgive his actions of faking to worship other gods as the King which whom he served, served other gods, and not God himself."

"Why would God show such grace to an evil man bent on destroying others' lives," asked Dr. Remy, "because God has more grace than we can ever truly think about. The story itself has so many theological wrestling about the Christian faith the reader has to deal with. The same thing with addiction, some things will never make sense, and you as the lover have to be content with not knowing why."

"Just like the book of Job," I replied, "no matter what religion you read the text in, the wisdom is given that no one knows why bad things happen to good people."

"Stop with your college boy logic," Dr. Remy said as she sat back down in front of me, "I need the romance in you. I need your D'Artagnan to Gwen's Constance Bonacieux"."

"The hero falls for a love that can never be," I replied

"And yet, he still pays Constance a reverence like no other," Dr. Remy said, "by the way, Mr. Writer, I know what you are doing with Gwen's name in your writings."

"Which is?" I asked, laughing cause I knew she figured it out

"Gwen is a name your ex-lover would understand if this story ended up in her hands," Dr. Remy replied as she sipped on a glass of water, "Gwen is a welsh feminine name and means white, holy. So you do see Gwen as your lady of light. But it is also short for Guinevere. And according to the King Arthur tale, "A Light In Guinevere's Garden," a story of unacquainted love."

"Guinevere falls madly in love with Arthur's best knight, Lancelot," I replied, " and they know they can never be together, even though they spent one magical night together. A passion in time, to be forever locked away never to be revisited, ever again."

"You know there are stories where Guinevere leaves Arthur for Lancelot," Dr. Remy said, " and lives peacefully in a life of poverty on a small farm outside England."

"There are also stories where Lancelot never slept with Guinevere and found the holy grail," I replied with a laugh, "and other stories where he betrayed Arthur further and burned down Arthur's righteous kingdom to the ground."

"Then you are truly Jason Blood, in this metaphor," said Dr. Remy, "and you need to master your demon of anger that awoke from this unacquainted love."

I was shocked that Dr. Remy knew of the Jason Blood reference. In modern comics, Jason Blood was the new name Lancelot went by after he was cursed by Myrlin with a bloodthirsty demon for Lancelot's insurrection against Arthur when Lancelot tried to overthrow King Arthur so that he could have Guinevere as Arthur's wife.

And so, Jason Blood must learn how to live a peaceful life so that the demon attached to his soul can never hurt anyone. But this metaphor sank Dr. Remy's point further into my soul.

"The aftermath of loving an addict at times," Dr. Remy said, "leaves a demon of anger, despair, and unwanting. A demon that must be slain with mercy and grace. Or forgiveness can never happen. and without forgiveness, no peace will come to you."

"How do you know so much about literature, and when I am pointing to things in my writing, doc'?" I asked with genuine curiosity.

"Being both a psychologist and therapist at times," Dr. Remy said, "I study people on a deep level, and to do that, you are drawn to literature as a philosopher would. As you and I both study people, just from different viewpoints."

"So, after I write about this therapy session, what do you want me to write about?" I asked

"Too early to write about Sam," Dr. Remy said, "I need you to trust me, so next session, I will share a close story with you, and you'll share about Sam, deal?"

"Deal," I replied

"So, focus on what you and Gwen's unique sexual nature," Dr. Remy instructed, "I need your brain heightened again; doing this will give you a type of exposure therapy that will have major benefits later on. After that, share in that primed moment, when you were there through one of Gwen's comedowns. Be honest with both her lady of the light and her lady of the dark. Share two stories of her wild nature, and then go into the dark moment. Because before delving into her dark side, you'll need the strength from her good side to get through it. After you do this, share when Gwen's caring nature was there when you needed her. I need you to build the path that walks you through the yin and yang of Gwen. To see Gwen's highs, lows, so you can understand her soul."

"Ok," I replied

"This should help you learn more of Gwen, in a way your heart has never seen before," Dr. Remy said, "then, I'll share my story after."

"Then, you will have me open about Sam, won't you?" I asked

"When you are ready, yes," Dr. Remy replied.

"When will we stop journaling about Gwen?" I asked

"When you can differentiate between the woman you love and the demon that holds her captive," Dr. Remy replied, "it's possible you met Gwen on a cycle and not her true path of sobriety. Gwen could have bounced from lover to lover, trying this religion or that school of spiritual thought, tried this job or that business, and because of her addictive behavior, it all failed every time."

This hit hard with me. The reason I knew this to be accurate, Gwen must have started three business ventures before I met her. Gwen even tried some investment ideas, and all failed. Plus, the lovers before me poured time and money into Gwen, and they all ended horrifically. Loving Gwen properly is hard work.

So, I made a vow during this therapy session. I was going to learn how to love Gwen properly and understand her addiction from a sincere, consecrated love point of view. Everyone deserves grace, which meant I needed to learn of Gwen as I had never known her before.

Dr. Remy left the kitchen and, for a brief moment, came back with a compilation of Jack Kirby's stories of Jason Blood and his demon Etrigan.

"Knowing your patient is key to helping save your patient," Dr. Remy said, "a small gift, as I knew you'd see this metaphor within yourself. It's possible Jack Kirby created Etrigan as a way of understanding the struggle within himself."

"Kirby did this a lot with his creations," I replied as I took the book. " The Eternals was about Jack's struggles with what he used to believe and what he wanted to believe now. Jack believed Vietnam was a bad idea even though being a World War 2 vet. His struggles with still believing in God, and did he believe in America like he used to?"

"Which is why from our last conversation," Dr. Remy replied," I knew Jack Kirby would be someone for you to latch onto. Kirby wrote the struggle within the self, Hemingway wrote about the battle with others viewed from the self."

"Learning my Yin and Yang, while understanding Gwen's," I said

"Yes," Dr. Remy confirmed, "because you unlocked something in Gwen no man could, her true nature within a passionate moment with a lover. So, when you write about the two stories of passion and love of Gwen? Write two of the times she wanted you as king."

"And when it comes the comedown story, write it from my Lancelot point of view," I said

"Exactly," Dr. Remy answered, " but as you do, you need to be honest about the dark side of yourself and the anger you felt when the drug binge emotional roller coaster ride stopped. Explore it in the romantic sense, to learn Gwen's demon properly. 'Cause believe it or not, Gwen loved the hell out of you, it is just her addiction got in the way."

"You got it, doc'," I said.

Before I left the kitchen, a thought bounced hard in my head, that I needed an answer to,

"Why do addicts in their cycles," I asked, " sometimes get hyper-religious, or when they get completely sober, become very strict in religious practice?"

"Some say it's because of the addictive nature of an addict always overdoing things," Remy replied, "I believe it more than that."

"Ok, so what's your thought?" I asked

"Let's use your Gwen, for example," Dr. Remy replied

"I'm listening," I replied

"Did Gwen have a disdain for a religion?" Dr. Remy asked

"Yeah, " I said, "anything Christian. When we had our first getaway, she pointed at a church and said I could never worship that, then pointed at my crotch and said I would rather worship that. But in a more vulgar way."

"So Gwen was hurt by that religion at some point," Dr. Remy said, " and new-age thinking nor Buddhism didn't work as you two broke up. So, given what little I know of her, she could have turned to a stricter religion like Muslim for a time because of her sister's boyfriend."

"Ok, what makes you think that?" I asked

"We'll, addicts want a normal life," Dr. Remy replied, " And Vickie bought the two-house farm for both Gwen and the younger sister. Which implies Gwen and the younger sister are thick as thieves."

"That's actually deeply true," I replied, " Gwen once showed me family pictures where she and her sister were taking turns to double Breastfeeding their boys to help the other one rest."

"So, the next religion she would explore would be Muslim," Dr. Remy said, " because of a deep bond with her sister, she would be influenced to try that religion to help bring order to her chaotic nature. Pray God gives them that order if true. I'm just giving you my educated theory."

"Your theory makes sense. We are communal beings by nature. That's why humans have created social structures and political systems," I said, "we need to belong to a group of some sort. We need healthy human interaction to be stable individuals."

"Which is why, Human nature, when in a good state, craves order from chaos," Dr. Remy replied, " addiction breeds chaos and dismay. So when trying to sober up, addicts need to reach for a higher power to help them bring their life back from the chaos and back into order."

"Thanks, doc'," I replied, "you gave me another piece of the puzzle of Gwen I was missing."

"You're welcome; see you Friday. Write well, and write honestly," Dr. Remy said, "Also, to give you hope, this therapy, this writing, is helping you draw something special into your life. Your holy grail, dear Lancelot, is coming— when you prove yourself worthy of holding it in your hands so you can drink from its sacred wine."

"I pray so doc'," I said, "I pray so."

Again, I was about to the leave the kitchen when a thought crossed my mind that I needed answers to.

"Doc'," I asked, "how do you know some of Gwen's unique sex life wasn't apart of her addictive nature or driven by it when it came to the dark stuff she wanted us to try? I know she cheated on me a few times when she was on a binge."

"Through the way she went about it," said Dr. Remy, "reading about how your wedding night went down versus how your relationship started, Gwen didn't let her real colors shine until she felt you were safe. The outfit you described that she wore that night, is not normal lingerie."

"What do you mean?" I asked, "most women dress sexy for special occasions."

"Sure, I'll give you that," said Dr. Remy, "but she mailed you her favorite underwear, which hinted at that she was a particular type of person. After receiving the package you could of freaked out, but didn't. Then you joined her for sex on a balcony without any drugs in her system or yours. Then your wedding night she wore lingerie that is being described as what an exhibitionist would've worn and you even hinted that the way she talked in a moment of passion, is very dirty and very wild; which means you definitely cleaned it up a bit. And in those times, in those moments, you both were sober and you gave no hint to her wanting to get high before hand. So Gwen is a wild woman in bed by her pure nature. It's just unfortunate her unaddressed addiction to cocaine corrupted what sex should have been for you two at certain times."

"That makes sense," I said

"I mean, it took time and planning to do the things she did with you," said Dr. Remy, "Gwen was a party girl addict. Meaning things driven by her addiction were impulsive and not thought all the way through. But when it came to you, everything was articulate and well planned out. Gwen was studying you to learn you. Gwen got her body pierced because you admitted to having a body piercing before. She asked which pantie she wore you liked the best. You showed enough signs to Gwen that made her trust she could be her true self with you. Something she probably repressed a lot. Also, after Hawaii she stopped doing drugs and yet, her wild sex didn't stop."

"Yeah," I said,

"How long was she clean for after Hawaii?" Dr. Remy asked

"Eight months," I admitted

"And Gwen never attacked you to go out and party?" Dr. Remy asked

"No," I said, "we just focused on me moving to Australia and building a life together."

"Then their you have it," Dr. Remy said, "Gwen was fighting for you, just as much as you were fighting for her. Which means Gwen saw she was tearing the only man who truly loved her, apart. And for a time, Gwen came alive and wanted her husband. Gwen wanted your real love and wanted you to accept her for who she really was. Unfortunately Sam's death caused her to have a horrible relapse that broke you both, which we will get into in later therapy sessions. Gwen fought hard for your love, and almost beat her addiction because of how much she knew you loved her."

Again Dr. Remy let her powerful words sink into my heart to heal me on another level.

"The other thing," Dr. Remy said in a concerned voice, "Because you need to hear it. Gwen's party side was a lot darker than you realize. That cocktail of bad coke you talked about? Means Gwen probably didn't know if she was coming or going. Which means, some of the cheating moments in Gwen's life, possibly weren't real cheating. It is highly possible that Gwen was chemically raped by more men than just the one man you told me about. Not saying person who takes ecstasy and cocaine doesn't know they might sleep with someone, 'cause they are very aware of the possibility. But at some point in an addicts life, chemical inspired sex and rape, begin to blur together, where sex just becomes sex. Which means Gwen probably felt dead inside. And then here you come along, and treat her like a gentleman? You probably weigh heavier on her heart then you realize. Did Gwen cheat on you, yes. But when did she cheat versus when it was against her will, you'll never know. Again, give her mercy."

"Fuck," I said as Dr. Remy's words beat into my soul.

"Love is never easy, Cliff," said Dr. Remy, "it is messy, it is complicated. The world is held together, really it is, held together, by the love and passion of the few. You can go to any city in any country, and find a valid reason to be angry with someone to the point of hate. But realize everyone you pass on the street is also you. They are you. You have the power to become just like the people who hurt you, or transcend them with love guided by grace and mercy. Of course your love affair with Gwen was a fiery romance you never saw coming. Passion happens. What you do with that memory now will decide if you are a bitter man or a great man. And I truthfully believe you are a great man and you want to forgive Gwen cause like it or not, she still holds the keys to your heart."

"And how do I get that piece of me back?" I asked

"By not allowing the devil to change you," said Dr. Remy, "the demon of Gwen's addiction destroyed you, and hurts many aspects of Gwen's life. So if you still submit to the rage inside your heart, understand you are beating Gwen's memory from a health issue she has no power over. If you truly believe Christ died for your sins- past, present, and future- and you are made in God's image? Then follow his footsteps, and take Gwen's sins against you as the price of loving her properly, so her sin against you doesn't effect anymore people in your life now. One of the aspects of your theology you are neglecting, Jesus died for your sins also so your sins wouldn't harm other people. Because pain is like a stone being thrown into a pond, the ripples become a wave on the shore line. And you isolating and hiding from the world while you slowly kill yourself is the byproduct of Gwen's sin against you still effecting your life. You don't think your family misses you? Or the friends you have miss getting a phone call from you? Forgiving Gwen will save your family and other relationships in your life. Being a Good man is hard, Cliff. The hardest thing in the world. But it is the good of the few that keeps this world from being swallowed by the pain and misery that is life."

"Family is an honorable man's love," I said as Dr. Remy's words sank deeper in my soul.

"Dead Poet's Society," laughed Dr. Remy, "that is a great film with a lot of great teachings. Now it is time for you to learn it's truth instead of quoting its speech, by living it, Cliff. Give Gwen's love meaning, and you will get your keys back. And as simple as it sounds, it will be the hardest thing that you have ever done."

"And how do I do that?" I asked

"By really looking into why is Gwen the love of your life?" Dr. Remy asked, "More importantly, what life lesson did you not learn from your Grandmother? She made sure you and your siblings didn't see your Grandfather at his lowest, yet, fought hard for her marriage though he was unfaithful and not a good man. What do you think you are missing from your Grandmother's life lesson that you need to know now with your personal struggle with Gwen?"

This therapy session was brutal but it helped reframe a lot of conflict in my soul.

Chapter 14

"A Wild Story"

Therapy today had my heart really focusing on my Grandparents in a new light. It also really opened my eyes to how Gwen studied me to give me happiness. The tattoo on Gwen's ass was a birthday gift I didn't pay attention to. Gwen asked me to draw her a heart tattoo, and when I did, Gwen then asked how I spell my whole first name.

I had no idea what that crazy love of mine did until she called me and gave signs she was in pain. Then it clicked what Gwen had done. The next thing I knew, when she got home, Gwen sent me very sexy photos of my tattoo. Why, out of all her lovers, why she chose to do this for my birthday, I don't know. All I know is it made me feel alive and wanted as I have never felt before. Which is why every time Gwen wanted to be intimate in her unique way, I thought I owed her that piece of myself. Gwen made me her world. That's why I could never tell her no.

Moreover, my Grandparents' story runs deep parallels. I barely started piecing together. We do attract things in our lives of what we are or have grown to be.

Grandpa moved out of his house at 14 and started being an entrepreneur. Grandpa began with a paper route first and found out he was a good salesman. Grandpa raised enough money and created an appliance repair store. That's when he met his first wife, and when they divorced, his ex-wife got all the businesses from Grandpa.

So Grandpa moved out of Arizona and came to California. And it is here in California where Grandpa made himself rich from building a new business. Also, Grandpa met Grandma, who just got out of a bad marriage with her ex, as Grandma's ex-husband was a gambler and womanizer, which sadly cost Grandma her chain of pizza parlors.

Grandma was there to help Grandpa to build his business. And Grandma, for Grandpa's birthday, helped Grandpa buy his first plane so he could learn to fly. Then came the snake in the grass that almost destroyed Grandpa.

The snake's name was Ellen. Ellen started in my grandfather's business as a salesperson but later became my grandfather's secretary. It's while Ellen was his secretary that Ellen used to lace my grandfather's coffee with speed. Before Grandpa knew it, he became the monster he never thought he would become. I genuinely believe prison saved my Grandfather's life.

My Grandparents' story gets crazier, though. When Ellen was dying of aides from the life she lived, my Grandmother moved her into her house while Grandpa was in prison and gave her a good life to pass on from. After that, when Grandpa got out, my grandparents adopted Ellen's son David so he would go into the foster care system.

David still lives on my Grandparent's horse ranch in the granny house. And when I asked Grandma why the hell she did this for a woman who tried to destroy her family, Grandma simply said:

"There is enough darkness in this world, boy, and some people get lost in it. And the only way to save someone from being lost is to be the light they need to come back home."

To this day, Grandpa worships Grandma; it's like he is wrapped around her finger. Grandma used to joke about Grandpa too, as Grandma is originally from Ireland, she would say

"I came to America for a holiday and fell in love with an American Cowboy who I had to raise to be a gentleman. Best investment of my life."

I was kicked out of my mother's house at a young age and married young for some dumb reason. Had my daughter. Then we divorced while I was deployed in Afghanistan, and yeah, my ex-wife took everything.

Gwen got away from her child's father as he was cheating on her and cared more for fun than the family. Well, according to Gwen, I don't know his side of the story. It's none of my business. And Gwen would take her Holiday time to see me, and I would take mine to see her.

I basically relived my grandparent's story with slight changes, which is powerful but weird. Grandma was Irish, and Gwen was Asian Australian. I was going to move to Australia, and Grandma visited California and never left. Grandparents always ran successful businesses. Gwen's companies always failed. Gwen struggled with coke, and Grandpa struggled with meth.

And sadly, I did not live up to my Grandmother's standard of being a light bearer for the family I was trying to have.

Which is also probably why I worked as a social worker to get addicts off drugs for a while if I am to be honest. Addicts, at times, don't realize how mortally bad they wound a person. So I was trying to be the light to bring them home. And yet, I was living a double life with this.

Every day I would go into the world to make it better than where I found it. The work was amazing. However, the dark halls of my house felt empty, and no matter how hard I worked myself into the ground to save people, Gwen's memory would never go away. Some nights I wanted to hate Gwen so bad but couldn't. Other nights I would drink until my brain couldn't think so that I wouldn't think of Gwen.

But like the old saying goes: a man takes a drink, and then another until the drink takes the man.

This makes me wonder, though. How many people actually self-reflect to see who influenced their life to attract the people in it, and try to study one's deep self to see where parallels between people match and where they differ. I am finding this to be a unique tool to discover who I am and why Gwen meant so much to me in my life.

My mind is racing on which stories are wise to share. As I explore what Gwen was, so many moments come to mind that gave me culture shock. Our love life didn't just encompass great sex, yet, if I were honest, Gwen is the only woman in my life that made sex feel like home. Others made sex feel fun and exciting, but Gwen gave it in a way as to make me feel as if I belonged.

So between our times apart, when we would endlessly FaceTime each other, I would always say, "Being with you, and not being with you, is the only way I have to measure time."

Then, in a lovely moment, she'd always reply, "I'll see you when I see you."

In the long months of our love affair, though we were content, there was a different longing with Gwen than I have ever had with anyone else. And in retrospect of those divine moments of longing, I learned a powerful truth about love. I knew I was born, and I would someday die, so in between was mine. So, I chose the love of Gwen with an internet dinner date than going and getting piss drunk rowdy with the boys. And she, for the most part, would do the same. It was a convenient clock between love and our time.

Though, I must admit, when things would get passionate in our flirtatious texts, I could sense Gwen pushing for more in our relationship, as she wanted to be free of something. As if whatever Gwen pretended to be with others, she didn't want to be with me. Gwen would say dirty jokes in front of the right friends when we hung out that were pretty extreme. But as time wore on, I saw the reality underlying those jokes when Gwen wanted to give me a private show, talk dirty to me, or have sex.

During my workday, Gwen would send naughty memes that showed a woman servicing a man or a man going behind a woman and devilishly seducing her. Sometimes I do admit, Gwen sent me active screen memes made from porn. Not every day or every time we texted, but when my workday was long, and she wanted to say, "I am waiting at home, for you."

Then one time, Gwen and I were talking about things one night, and during our conversation, she told me of a business idea she and her French neighbor Molly were thinking of doing.

"We are thinking of a sex line," Gwen told me

I didn't know how to react. As this was the time I was learning, Australians, and Europeans, had different views on sex than us Americans.

"Why?" I asked nervously

"Because it sounds like an easy side business venture," Gwen laughed, "Molly and I don't have to go around showing our you-ha's to every Tom, Dick, and Harry. We just talk. They don't see what they look like, and we don't see them. So, no real risk of others finding out."

"I'm sorry, I don't know what to say," I legit told her because I was nervous and confused.

Being raised in small-town America, even though I had my fair share of lovers and done crazy stuff with them, my mindset was still archaic. But I was willing to hear Gwen out as I loved her.

"Hubby, we are born alone, we die alone, yeah?" said Gwen, "and then people drop a whole bunch of rules on you to make you forget that fact. But I never do; that is why I do what I want. Which is why the fat cunt bitch soccer mom hates me so much. Even though she knows all she has to do to keep her man happy is open her legs once in a while or give the poor bastard a head job. Because if she did, maybe her husband would stop eye fucking me three aisles back every time they got to the supermarket. Yet, women like me get slut shamed by people like her. Why? Because real women who actually control their own bodies, never follow anyone's rules who are lazy and afraid of being real."

"Have you ever thought of this kind of work before?" I asked, generally curious.

"Of course, when I was a bit younger," Gwen said, "when the boy's father and I were on a break. I advertised on an adult website to make money. It was crazy the amount of money I could have made if I didn't chicken out."

"Why did you chicken out?" I asked

"I don't know," Gwen answered, "I had outfits picked for the client, and the prices were set for the encounter he wanted. And the escrow account that acted as the middle man between us showed huge numbers in the account if the date went well. Then I started to talk with the boy's father again, the dumb shit."

"How much money were you going to make?" I asked

"The site was aimed at countries that didn't allow adult entertainment services," Gwen replied, "that had people coming to Australia for pleasure. So, I would've made ten grand for a week's worth of work. And trust me, I would have made good money; I would have sucked his shit good to keep him coming back."

And this is the very moment the real Gwen started coming through to me when Gwen began to show how wild she really was. Because now Gwen had a lover nonjudgmental to what she wanted to try.

Though I do admit, Gwen did try me first to see how touchy I was on the sexual taboo thing.

One time, while working the night shift for my transition job, I got home showered, got in bed, and called Gwen. Gwen was wearing a nun outfit where the back was cut open to where I could see she was wearing a black thong. I admit it made me uncomfortable, yet, I went along with it somewhat. I allowed her to strip and talk dirty, but I wasn't into it. But I allowed her to take it as far as she wanted.

The show was short because Gwen could see how exhausted I was, and we bid adieu, so I could get some rest. When I woke up, Gwen sent many photos and videos of herself in the nun outfit playing with her toy. And all I texted to her when I woke up was,

"Good morning, wifey. Thank you for the yummy things to wake up to," because I did not want her thinking what she did was in vain. I just wanted Gwen to be herself.

That was the firecracker that finally popped off to Gwen's sexual revelation to me.

To give context, this all happened after Gwen and I had our Hawaii spiritual marriage. That night, I should have seen who Gwen really was. However, I didn't. I could sense Gwen was a wildfire of a woman; I never thought she was this far into exploring sex until after we married.

And come to think of it, I think Dr. Remy is right. Gwen opened up to who she was because if I was going to be her husband, she had to be as honest with me as I was trying to be with her. Plus, I am the only man who put a ring on her finger. No man before me ever gave Gwen this level of commitment before. And honestly, Gwen's fascination with exploring sex in her unique way opened the door to a hilarious story Gwen, and I will share for a lifetime.

One night I was reading a book, and Gwen texted me on her lunch break.

"Baby, I want to talk to you about something serious," Gwen texted.

"Ok," I texted back

My heart got extremely nervous, so I rushed to call her because that usually starts a break-up conversation.

"Is everything ok, baby?" I asked

Gwen laughed, "of course, you bloody yank. I want to ask you something because there is something I need to try. But I can't talk about it here, so I'll text you."

As soon as I hung up, my heart stopped racing, but something interesting from Gwen came in my text messaging app that made it race even more.

"I want to have a threesome," Gwen texted.

My heart skipped in excitement and confusion for a moment. If I were, to be honest, for a long moment, as again, I had conflicts inside of me due to my upbringing. But then, my memory reminded me how hypocritical I was being.

What is the difference between double-teaming a lover vs. a threesome? Honest. Not much. One, people take turns with one lover and leave when done. A threesome is two people enjoying the lover at the same time. A person still gets to have two lovers in one night, in both instances.

I understand now from this relationship I had with Gwen men get to this freedom with sex that women just don't get. Why we put constraints on women, I just don't know. But I loved Gwen, and I didn't want her in a marriage with me if it meant she wouldn't be allowed to be her true self. That was my way of thinking about it back then. I don't know if I would have made the same choices now. But I made them of my own free will to make Gwen feel loved and accepted.

So I texted back, "let me know when you want to do it."

Oddly enough, one of the friends called me, with whom I had the double team with, and sought advice, as I was nervous. For the sake of her protection, I will call her Charlotte.

"Hey Cliff, what are you doing?" Charlotte asked me

"Planning something, I never thought I do," I replied

"What's that?" Charlotte asked

"My new wife wants a threesome," I told her

"So?" Charlotte replied, "It's no different than what you and I did at my welcome home party with what's his name. Besides, I had one recently, and they can be fun with the right people."

"Ok," I said to her

"It's not a crime to love sex, Cliff," Charlotte said, "your wife just wants to try something before she is too old to do it. Let her, man."

I still felt weird as this was something normal married couples don't do. Usually people do crazy things like this before marriage to get it out of the youthful system. Marriage is a place to build a life with someone. But like I said, once married in our own spiritual way, that is when Gwen revealed her real self.

"I don't know of any other person in Australia, " I texted Gwen, "so, I am going to trust you to choose the person. Just make sure this won't come back to haunt us."

Gwen didn't text me for a long time as she was working, but the moment she got off work, I got this text from her-

"Thank you, hubby. I have an idea, calling."

Again I was in shock seeing Gwen's mindset was going but I followed it, to see where she wanted to take it.

So when the phone call came through, I picked up.

"Hubby, you there," Gwen asked

"Yes," I said

"I want a threesome with another girl, someone we don't know to be safe," Gwen told me

"Ok, how are we going to do that?" I asked

"We'll just go to a brothel while you visit, it be $500 or so," Gwen replied

At this point, is when I found out brothels were legal in Australia. And I was deathly afraid of hookers because of my modern American upbringing. And I really wanted to impress Gwen, who obviously did homework on the idea in case I happened to say yes to her crazy plan. I mean, how else would Gwen know how much a threesome would cost in a brothel?

"Ok," I choked out

Gwen laughed with a calming laugh.

"It's going to be ok hubby," Gwen assured me, "We'll go in, have fun, and have a memory of something we both have never done before. Well, kind of."

"Ok," I laughed, "go on, tell me."

"Few years back when I first left dumb shit for the last time," Gwen said, "I went on a girl vacation with my best mates to Vietnam. We partied, and I don't know what happened exactly, but one of my besties saw me last riding on a Vespa with two other women. I woke up the next morning naked in their bed. So I want to know what it's like to remember something that free and not feel judged."

So realizing my new wife struggled with a bi-curious question about her own sexual identity? As crazy as it sounds (wrong or right), my heart just said do it, give her the experience that she feels that she needs to know. I can't imagine what it's like to feel locked in an image that you're just not like Gwen did.

And given the fact Gwen comes from a strict cultural background where her own culture would disown her if they knew Gwen's natural sexual appetite? Especially hearing how Gwen's older relatives who raised her talked negatively about gay and bisexual people, it must be hard for Gwen to be Gwen.

"I'll follow you on whatever you want to do," I told her

"I'll let you do whatever you want with her," Gwen said confidently, "just don't take your eyes off me, as you do it."

"Yes ma'am, I promise," is what I said, but in my mind, I was like "is this really fucking happening?"

Gwen found a nice brothel about two cities away from where she lived, and away from Sydney. This way we could go in and have our experience and never ever get caught. Because no one we knew would be in this particular city anyway, it was a long drive away. I felt like an accomplice to a crime about to be committed at the time.

While driving to the brothel, Gwen was excited like a teenage girl sneaking out to see a boyfriend she wasn't supposed to see. Gwen, no joke, talked to my penis at one point as a joke, and said, "Today is a good day, 'cause you're getting two pussies!"

When I say Gwen was acting childish due to excitement, I mean it. I on the other hand was freaking out. I had a war of ideas going on inside me, that looking back were pretty funny-

"Are we going to use a condom? Is it right to sleep with a hooker? I barely know what to do with one woman, what the hell am I going to do with two?"

Meanwhile, when we got to the city Gwen wanted to make herself perfect for this moment. Gwen got completely nude waxed, and then shopped for the perfect bra and panties to wear for her experience, even cut her hair just right and dolled her make up more than normal. Gwen then checked to see if the small recording device she brought was charged. Gwen wanted to own this moment, and truly experience absolute freedom, while I, on the other hand, was freaking out inside.

And yes, I am not joking, Gwen wanted video proof for herself to keep, so that if we broke up for some reason, she would have a memory of this moment. Gwen wanted proof in her life that someone at some point allowed her to be Gwen.

During the pantie shopping, Gwen showed me the brothel's website, and I did see pictures of beautiful girls posing quite nicely. And with it, I took a deep breath, and allowed the images to confirm in my mind what was about to transpire.

Gwen was ready, and looking forward to our little adventure. We took a deep breath, and drove to the brothel.

Once we got into the brothel, we were greeted by a very nice lady and she asked us "what are you two lovers here for?"

"A threesome," Gwen said in a calm confident voice.

"Of course," the madam of the house replied, "follow me please."

Inside the brothel, it looked like a rich person's house. Fine furnishings, classic wafted drapes, the designer put time, effort and a lot of money to make it look like a high end establishment.

The madam of the house walked us into a room, through a set of oak doors that once inside, looked like a gentlemen's cigar room.

"Have a seat," the Madam said gently, "and your lady will be in momentarily to discuss prices, and conditions of your request. Meanwhile, pour yourselves a brandy if you fancy, while you wait."

So we had a seat on the two luxury chairs, and Gwen poured me a small brandy in a brandy snifter glass. I swirled it a bit before sipping it, Gwen was obviously trying to keep me comfortable, as she now doubt noticed my hand shake.

When I tasted the brandy, it was stiffer than others I drank before, meaning it was cheap. Good brandy's are usually smooth with no real harsh bite. Which should have been a foreshadowing of what was to come, but I was scared stupid at this moment.

Then walked in our lady from another set of oak doors adjacent within the room of the oak doors we walked into the room from.

Both Gwen and I were shocked in absolute horror as our chosen lady that was the only one in the brothel to do a threesome, was an old hag father time road hard as hell, and put away wet. Woman had some "fuck me" miles, Gwen and I didn't want to know about.

The lady sat across from us with fishnet stockings that couldn't hide her sagging thighs, though they tried. The corset the lady wore looked at it was struggling to keep everything together, and then came the forsaken moment my young eyes wish they had never ever seen. The lady crossed her legs in front of us revealing she was wearing crotchless panties that exposed the fact if I ever tried to ride her in any way, my mini me was going to be a hotheels mini car being thrown down a New York subway tunnel. I was frozen stiff.

I was so scared this was about to go down, I choked down every drop of that cheap brandy in one gulp as the Lady began to talk with the worse lisp I ever heard coming with someone obviously wearing dentures.

"Well," she said, "Nice to meet you. "

"You too as well," Gwen replied

"My fee will be $300," The Lady said, "Which I believe to be a fair offer if this is your first time. It is your first time isn't it?"

"Yes," Gwen said with a gentle smile on her face.

"I have seen this type of experience strengthen marriages if certain rules are kept at all times," the Lady said, "I will let you know what I will do and not do for you, and what you will be allowed to do to me, in return you will share your boundaries. Once inside my bed chamber, these rules are God. Breaking these rules ends the playtime, no matter how far we went or didn't go, deal?"

"Yes, we agree," Gwen said.

"I do allow fisting," the Lady said

And at this point my brain checked out as it thought, "Who the fuck would want to, it looks like that damn thing would swallow person whole so you could spit them out your back end!"

Gwen looked as she was intently listening to this Lady while I, on the other hand, wanted to break the brandy glass, and lobotomize myself with one of its glass shards, so I wouldn't remember a thing that was about to transpire.

Then when the woman was done, Gwen calmly shook the Lady's hand properly, and said, "I am going to take my husband to lunch first, pencil us in for within the hour. See you soon, ta'."

As soon as we left from inside the brothel and were close to Gwen's car, I couldn't hold it back any longer.

"FUCK NO!" I whispered very wildly in shock of what was happening.

"Thank God," Gwen said, "I was afraid you were just going to want to do it anyway, so I was taking us to the lunch place first to get drunk first."

"Why on earth," I said, "would I ever want to lay with that unholy mess of nightmares?"

"Because you have a dick," Gwen quipped back, "and most men don't care which woman those things get stuck in."

Needless to say, Gwen and I went down the street to a small mom and pop bar and grill, and got tanked for lunch until our speech slurred. Our lunch break was 100% a liquid feast of: martini's for starters, a shot gunned beer, a few tequila shots, topped all off with a two finger pour of the strongest whiskey they had, that tasted like a lifetime of self loathing and bad decisions. The kind of whiskey that burns your throat and punches the wind out of your lungs.

Looking back at this story, I see what you mean doc'. When the real Gwen wanted to explore things, she took her time and planned things out to the letter. Gwen is never going to fit the mold of what accepted society is, even clean for 100 tears.

The times Gwen used sex as a weapon to get high, it was always aggressive, mean. And when I really think on it, irrational. I understand sexy foreplay where lovers use wax, and toys. That I understand. But when Gwen had a craving, she wanted the foreplay to be uncomfortable for me, so I would stop, which then gave her addiction the excuse to get high.

The real Gwen didn't want it that rough, just kinky. But the addiction within her lied in what Gwen actually wanted, so the addiction could be fed its pound of flesh. And it is also why when she come home after a binge she could never look me in the eye. Gwen's addiction was pushing me away so it could steal another piece of her soul. And as I stayed through those episodes, Gwen had her mood swings, but, she started more and more to be home.

Because of my dedication Gwen was cutting cocaine addiction cold turkey, and in my anger, I have completely forgot this about her. Gwen didn't go through therapy, and didn't take any psychiatric medications.

In the eight months of her sober life with me, Gwen must of felt emotional hell. I know this because sometimes Gwen admitted to using anti-depressants when the come down was too rough from a night of binging. Which brings a whole other question to mind.

Why didn't Gwen go get medication to help regulate her emotions again from the doctor, if she was so serious about quitting?

Chapter 15

"Knowing Gwen"

After our plans of a wild romantic soirée finished burning to the ground and we sobered up a bit, I did what any gentleman would do when a date doesn't go as planned; I took Gwen shopping. I wanted to cheer Gwen up. Today was supposed to be the day Gwen would get to be herself, with no one judging or asking questions. I was just being in the moment and accepting her. Plus, I had $5k of cash on me; seeing Gwen smile after that horrific dumpster fire just seemed right.

For Gwen, it started out innocent at first. We looked at furniture and cooking stuff she liked, and then she really opened up on what she wanted to shop for: clothes and sexy clothes.

I get it. I am not the only man in world history to take his woman shopping after a world-crushing event. However, I am good at analyzing stuff, and I knew Gwen felt defeated. I mean, three times, Gwen tried explaining this craving she wanted to experience this threesome idea, just once. So this was a brutal shut down to her yet again, not being able to be herself. Yet, this didn't change the fact Gwen craved exploring sexual relationships with a safe lover.

I stopped and got a book on world history stuff at the bookstore near the lingerie shop I took Gwen to. As Gwen tried on different thongs, g strings, and bras, in the changing area where I was not allowed, I read my book. This, of course, didn't detour Gwen from flirting with me.

My phone would vibrate ever so often to alert me that Gwen sent me a new sexy photo to see of lingerie she was trying on in her stall. What can I say? She knows how to grab a boy's attention.

In between Gwen's sexy texts and me trying to ensure no one was looking over my shoulder when I looked at them, I read something in the book that hit hard. Something I would maul over in the car ride home back to Gwen's house.

During the second world war was over, a body of a dead soldier was found with a note in his pocket that read:

"When the war is over, we will get married, and the earth will grow flowers like you, and your womb will carry the most beautiful girl in the universe."

I know people's best-laid plans lay waste in war, as many people don't make it back home to loved ones. But this letter this man wrote hit on a different level. Even as Gwen's spirits were picked back up and she was singing to George Michaels on the car stereo, this letter consumed my thoughts.

It really hit how fleeting life was. It showed how human beings make plans for tomorrow as they forget tomorrow never comes. We are only our existence—nothing more, nothing less. So, whatever we decide to do today is all that matters. I am mine, Gwen is Gwen', and each their own master. Fate loves the courageous. Because fate is whatever we make of it today.

So, when we got home, and we relaxed a bit, Gwen started modeling the various g strings, and thongs for me, in the bedroom.

I admit, though, as Gwen gave me a live strip show of various degrees, that soldier's love letter consumed my mind until something awoke in me.

I always knew where Gwen's sex toys and outfits were. They were in a locked chest at the foot of her bed. Gwen had it open as she knew she couldn't place some of the underwear in the underwear drawer that had her normal thongs she wore. Some of the lingerie was for sexual use and nothing else. And Gwen's two boys were very nosy, who, when she grounded them from cell phone usage, would sneak into her room and look for the cell phone. So Gwen's sex chest had two locks and kept everything about Gwen's sexual wants and desires locked away and hidden from such prying eyes.

In the chest, I saw Gwen's: ropes, handcuffs, collars, and leash, along with various spanking tools. As Gwen was putting on one of her new panties that I had just bought her, I instinctively placed the collar on Gwen's neck, and attached it to it.

"What are you doing, hubby," Gwen asked me with a devilish grin.

I didn't answer. I just handcuffed Gwen behind her back and led her by the leash out the bedroom naked. She was wearing nothing but blue lace panties, the leash I placed on her, and the handcuffs that bound Gwen's hands behind her back.

When we got to the couch in the living room, I made sure to gently jerk the chain to pull Gwen closer to me, Gwen moaned. The fire inside Gwen was being stoked. Her eyes began to burn with hunger.

I walked her to the sliding glass door at the back of her living room. The door curtains were drawn completely open, to where we could see truckers driving up and down the farm road just beyond her property line. I made Gwen stand there exposed, watching the truckers just drive on by, knowing, at any moment, all they had to do was look a little left or a little right, and they would see Gwen in all her glory.

Gwen began to pant hard, as she was getting turned on by the idea of getting caught. I really knew this when I slowly traced my hand down her stomach, past her pantie line, to Gwen's burning sweat spot. That's when I felt Gwen flutter like I never have before.

"Come," I said as I tugged the chain to lead away from the window.

Because I knew if I stood there any longer, the thrill would have faded for Gwen. So I walked her to the couch, and grabbed one of her throw pillows and placed the pillow before her.

"On your knees," I told her sternly as I gently pulled the chain in the direction I wanted her body to go.

As I slowly unzipped myself and watched Gwen's fire come truly alive. I don't know why I did it but I grabbed a handful of her hair to let her know I was in charge, and all Gwen could do is moan, "yes, daddy."

I placed myself slowly in Gwen's mouth, and played with her lips a bit as I did, and she played with me with her tongue. Gwen's fire became quite thirsting when she saw me pull out my cell phone to video her. It was if Gwen was attracted to sex that if caught would destroy her reputation. And a part of her at some level wanted to be seen and found out.

Every time I pulled out she would say wild things I never heard her say before, and no I am not sharing what she said. Some of it made me feel uncomfortable cause I never heard a woman talk like that in my life. Some of it turned me on. All that was on my mind was giving Gwen the excitement she longed for.

And Gwen, like the perfect adult film star, born for the role, knew how to look into my camera with a look that made me want her even more. So I uncuffed her hands, and bent her over the couch, and bagn spanking her with my hand.

"Oh daddy," Gwen moaned and begged, "please, I need it harder."

And the harder I spanked, the more into it Gwen became. To the point that by the time I placed myself deep inside her, Gwen had such an orgasm that I was left dripping wet, and she collapsed on the couch, as her body gave slight twitches. This was my Gwen, alive when sex was truly explored within it's greatest pleasures.

I was going to just clean up, and zip myself up and let Gwen have her moment. But, Gwen had other ideas. Gwen wanted to treat me like a king for finally giving her fire what it desired for so long.

Gwen sat me on her couch and pulled my pants down to my ankles, and left for her room, for a brief moment. When she returned she had an adult video in her hand and placed it in her dvd player.

As the film began, Gwen took my cell phone, and videoed herself saying, "this is how you treat a fucking man."

Gwen then placed me in her mouth and sucked me like I have never been before. It was so good, as my hand rested on the back of her head, it instinctively began grabbing a small ball of her hair as my release would come. And no, she did not stop, she just kept going.

As if Gwen knew a greater pleasure was coming, and wanted me to experience it. Gwen kept licking, sucking and swallowing until my divine moment came. And orgasm that made my brain feel warm like it was being massaged by warm water. My body couldn't help but go limp as the feeling of a warm blanket wrapped around my body, and my ejaculet felt like a warm gushing river that felt so good, my toes would curl.

As I lay limp, Gwen just crawled into my arms, and rested with me on the couch. I turned the tv off so we could rest in the silence.

And after my last therapy session, I wonder if this is what gave Gwen the strength to stop from reaching for a cocaine bag a week later. We got into an argument over the phone to where Gwen got so heated and said she was going to her sisters.

I naturally was on edge because I didn't know which sister. Was it the older sister who wanted Gwen clean, or was it the younger sister with the party boyfriend. Either way that night I promised myself to end everything with Gwen if she used that night.

Around one in the morning I got a phone call from Gwen that woke me from my not so restful beauty sleep, as I was tossing and turning all that night. And let me tell you, I was ready to end it as I picked up the phone.

It turned out to be a FaceTime call. As I allowed the call to come through, I could see the tears and shame in Gwen's eyes.

"I went to Vickie's, hubby," Gwen started, "and my sister was also there with her boyfriend. He gave me the bag, and I just couldn't do it. Truth is, I don't think I ever loved anyone before you. You make me want to be someone else. As I turned it down, he was shocked."

"Did Vickie know he brought drugs into her house?" I asked

"No," Gwen said, "Vickie can be so full of herself at times that she misses things about people around her."

"I am proud of you, I am very proud of you," I said because I was.

"I don't know what broke me, hubby, why I choose naughty things," Gwen said, "all I know is you make everything better. I can be me and be loved for me."

Gwen even asked if I wanted her to take a drug screen test and if I did, she would get one the next day. Something about this time, I knew I didn't need the proof. So when she calmed down from crying, she asked if we could FaceTime all night so she could watch me sleep. So I told her yes and left FaceTime open all night.

And when I woke up the next morning, I saw Gwen's face sound asleep. On her pillow was a t-shirt I had left behind on my last visit. It was if Gwen was using it to smell me, to feel me somehow. In fact for a month straight until our next meet up, Gwen wanted to do this every night. She just wanted to be close to me any way she could.

God, how did I get so angry to forget something like this.

Chapter 16

"The Lady In Black"

The truth is, Gwen had many comedowns while she and I were together. Gwen would have many hangovers where she slept in a friend's bathroom next to the toilet. And other times where she wasn't sober enough yet to go home after being on a 24-hour drug binge party with God knows who and saying things like:

"Hubby, calm down, yeah? It's in my system, but not in my system. I got my wits about me now."

Then Gwen would drive to her Uncles to pick up her kids and call me when they all three got home. During these long car rides from Sydney to her quiet farm life, anxiety, rage, and fear crippled me. Because every time I brought it up, how unsafe it was, it always spilled into an argument of epic proportions to where Gwen started weird tactics like gaslighting me.

I honestly didn't know what gaslighting was until I checked myself into this therapy program. I literally thought all the coke Gwen was using was destroying her short-term memory. To where she was emotionally compromised, and she didn't know what she had said, and it made her uncomfortable. But it was gaslighting; tactic addicts use to deflect from their dangerous behavior or not wanting to address it.

I wonder if we both were drawn to danger in a weird way. I mean, we met over the internet on a social media platform that doesn't exist anymore and started sexting each other and flying to see each other almost every month. Who I am now, I would not do any of this. Yet, for Gwen, I would have moved the world. Gwen got into me like no one has ever done.

There were times Gwen tried hiding that she had partied all night over the weekend, but her lies would find her. One can't hide coke nose too long as the person who used coke the night or day before is constantly snorting and blowing their nose. At least Gwen did after she used it.

And yes, I knew she probably cheated on me more than once when she was using; I was in love, not stupid. The problem I struggle with now is how many people took advantage of her while she was binging, and she was too scared to tell me?

Gwen tried to prove her faithfulness when she partied by calling me and not answering the phone, so I could overhear her turn down a would-be suitor. But this didn't happen every time. So, I believe it was either a guy she really didn't care for, or she wasn't tanked yet.

The reason I can say this in confidence is when Gwen was sober and trying to be my wife; her infidelities came to light in a not so pretty way as ex-lovers reached out to me. One was upset Gwen used him for a one-night stand and left him. And two reached out to me to mock me that they banged Gwen.

And after the therapy session today, looking back, the two guys who mocked me for sleeping with Gwen? The way Gwen reacted as this came about, she was terrified. Gwen's eyes looked sad and scared. Which makes my skin boil, and the rage in my heart wants to punch someone. It's possible those two jerks loaded Gwen up and used her.

What made me forgive Gwen when these things came to light was Gwen had been sober for four months. Gwen was trying everything in her power to prove she could be an honorable wife. Gwen even went as far as linking her phone to my phone somehow, so I knew where she was at all times. I never asked her to do it; she did it independently.

That, and though I was struggling with my faith at that time, I leaned into the teaching of found in Ephesians 5:25:

"Husbands, love your wives, just as Christ loved the church and gave himself up for her."

So I understand what was meant in therapy when Dr. Remy said about forgiving Gwen. But to live this verse as a man, a good man, how much love and forgiveness do you give before it gets abused?

Yet, I used this verse and tried to love her through what was going on. Because honestly, it felt like a trial to prove who I was so that Gwen could learn what real love was. And now that I think about it, Gwen changed drastically when I chose to stand with her after this.

Gwen never left home unless we both were together and going to a place together. Gwen even went as far as to delete the party friends from her phone and block them on social media. Looking back now through this writing, I can honestly say she fought hard to prove she was worthy of the chance I was trying to give her.

Still, there are things about Gwen that rub my soul the wrong way that I want to know the answers to but probably never will.

Before she and I became official, instead of flirty bed friends online, Gwen told me she was going to see a friend she met at the meditation retreat. And that in the following morning, she had a coffee date with the rancher guy her sister Vickie was trying to get her to pursue.

The night after, she rang me up, telling me that she probably wouldn't see the rancher again, and her friend from the meditation retreat was bad news. But said his house looked nice.

Months went by, and she said she met up with the guy, and he tried getting her to go to his place after a meet-up, but she didn't go to his house and saw pictures of the guy's home on his phone as he remodeled his living room. A month or so after that, she joked with me one night-

"I think I scared my sister's rancher friend away," Gwen laughed

"Why is that," I asked

"I was hungover during that coffee meet," said Gwen, "and I accidentally pulled a pair of used panties out of my purse when looking for my chapstick that I forgot I put in there."

Then after that, about two days went by; Gwen logged into my computer to chat with some friends and forgot to log back out. That's when I read a small string of texts between her and her girlfriend talking about how much she and Gwen drank and that the coke was really good this time. And yes, Gwen admitted to her friend that she slipped away from the party that night with the guy, but nothing happened. That the guy only wanted a notch on his belt, and Gwen left him dry.

So I allowed my curiosity to kick me in the gut and read this supposed guy friend's text. They were brief texts like "hey," "hi," and "what up." But it also had proof that Gwen lied about sleeping with the guy.

The guy said thank you for the experience and that it was fun snorting coke off her ass. And Gwen said it was a nice goodbye. Guess the dude was moving. The part that pissed me off and hurt me, though, I mean we were not serious until a week after this incident, so why lie about it?

Gwen's comedowns were brutal at times. Like an emotional whirlwind roller coaster where she couldn't handle stress or manage anger properly. She would use the silent treatment as punishment or scream mean things at you that she knew would cut you deep. For me, she would say disturbing things like

"Shooting guns makes you feel like a big man, baby killer?"

Only for her to swallow her pride and beg for forgiveness because she realized that the calm down made her an evil bitch. Dr. Remy was right; it was like dealing with Dr. Jekyll and Hyde. I couldn't believe the comedown of cocaine made this sweet woman an evil, vindictive person who spewed venomous words like a dragon breathing fire.

And I remember the one time when she confessed that her heart stopped while partying with her baby daddy in Vietnam, I asked-

"What happened?"

"I took too much of a Xanax to help with a comedown," said Gwen, "and my heart stopped. It happened two times before that."

"Aren't you scared your boys won't grow up without a mother?" I asked her

"No, if I die, it's my life, my problem," Gwen replied, as she couldn't grasp the trauma of her two baby boys growing up without a mother, whom they loved, just died one day.

Two bad comedowns come to mind as I write this chapter. The first real bad one came after Gwen did the dirty coke that was all over the news, that had been laced with meth and GHB (gamma-hydroxybutyric acid), also called "Easy Lay," as it is commonly used as a date rape drug. This dirty coke's come down was vicious on Gwen. Gwen screamed, cried, felt rage, and then went into dark depressions. And I, like a loving hubby, stayed up with her the whole night.

The other comedown that really sticks out in my mind is one where I literally thought Gwen had finally lost the plot.

Gwen called me in a frantic quiet voice and asked me, "Hubby?"

"Yes," I answered

"Do you hear the music?" she asked, crying

"No," I told her

"It's like a violin that keeps playing on repeat, and it won't stop," Gwen said, crying, "like an evil violin."

I admit at this time in my life; I struggled with what I believed. I saw more of the devil in Afghanistan than I ever did of God. So my belief in the supernatural was shaky at best at this juncture in my life. But, I got my bible and started reading Matthew 6:9 and praying over Gwen with it until she fell asleep.

Which honestly helped me restore my faith in God a little bit. As it felt God was healing Gwen from corrupted coke. And yes, I did call the ambulance for her, and she turned down medical help. And at that point, I was just lost. I didn't know what to do except just being there for her on the phone, FaceTiming her, as she went through the craziest emotional roller coaster I had ever seen a human being go through.

The following day when Gwen called, she confessed that she believed her farmhouse to be haunted. However, I didn't think Gwen's house was haunted. Even after Vickie's sage friend came over and told this elaborate story on how and why the house was haunted, she burned herbs through the house. They used crystals and tarot cards.

I tried to get Gwen to admit to Vickie it was probably her mind playing tricks on her the night before because she was loaded. Gwen kept insisting that she believed a ghost was in her house, and her coming down off of bad coke had nothing to do with her hearing creepy music all night long unless I prayed over her.

But I did what any sane borderline atheist who struggles in spiritual beliefs after the war would do, and I bought a medical book on cocaine addiction. There I found something out that turned my stomach.

Cocaine can cause paranoia and violent behaviors. Also, it is not uncommon for a cocaine addict to develop delusions, hallucinations, bipolar disorders, or have combined psychiatric disorders of various degrees after long-term use.

So it is highly possible that cocaine created mental instability within Gwen after a youthful lifetime of addiction.

And doc' I think you are right, especially after reading this chapter out loud, and seeing what thoughts I had to gather, in order to put the letter to the page, Gwen was possibly on a cycle of cleanliness when I fell in love with her. And not on her true path to sobriety.

Gwen tried and started three business ideas before me, and every time she had a fallout with a lover, she always ended up in her ex's bed with who she had children with, regardless if he had a girlfriend or not. And when we were together, Gwen had this mantra that used to annoy the piss out of me

"What you did before me, and what you do after me, I don't care. It's what you do, when you are with me, that I care about."

Which when she tried being sober, she always asked for forgiveness for saying it. Gwen trying to be sober was like a whole new person who believed in hope, love, and trust. Instead of living by passions, wants, and desires.

With this all being said, I am understanding the yin and yang of Gwen. Looking back as I write all this out, I am not writing of her comedowns from cocaine exactly. My heart is exploring all the reasons why she did cocaine and how drug-style party life robbed Gwen of a real existence within herself.

Gwen was lost in a world of no love. Growing up, Gwen didn't love herself because no one taught her what love actually was. And I can say this with confidence because of the night Gwen shared old picture albums with me about her past.

Vickie got to go to private schools and be taken by her Uncle. Gwen, on the other hand, was born in the refugee camps in Australia. So Gwen's and Vickie's lives are totally different. Gwen's Uncle tried to help them the best he could, but then her Uncle had two kids of his own and had to focus on them and his promise to Vickie.

Because Gwen's Uncle served in the American armed forces, he got benefits for his family from the American and Australian military. Like the Veteran Affairs loan, where Gwen's Uncle could buy a house with no money down and didn't have to pay closing costs or escrow costs of any kind with the house loan structured as to pay the loan at $500 a month against a $500k home. And the reason the VA loan is so cheap is cause the loan when accepted in certain areas in Australia. My home in Riverside, California, the veteran doesn't pay any property tax or house. The veteran can choose which house insurance company they want to go with or have no house insurance at all.

Also, this was back in the day in Australia. When I was buying a home in Australia, the laws drastically changed for me, and I would have gotten only a quarter of the stuff Gwen's Uncle was awarded. This is why when Gwen and I broke up, I moved to California because I got more benefits with my loan and G.I. bill than I would have by moving to Australia.

Plus, Gwen's Uncle was taught a certified trade of being a mechanic from the Navy Seals as well English. And Gwen's Uncle signed over his G.I. Bill, the fund that pays for American soldiers to get free college, passed to Vickie so she could go to the best private schools.

Gwen's parents sadly had to learn English as they went along in life. They couldn't work for Ford motor companies like Gwen's Uncle did because they didn't have the certifications. So Gwen's Dad worked as ranch hands on a farmers vegetable farm until he saved up enough to buy his own farm and started his own business. Which meant Gwen's dad left Monday morning out to the farmlands and didn't come home until Friday night for some heavy amount of years. Gwen's mom worked as a seamstress. From what I could understand, it was run like a sweatshop. Which meant Gwen's mom wasn't home until late at night. They were leaving Gwen oftentimes to take care of her and her other siblings.

And for school, Gwen went to a catholic school cause it was free to her parents as they were poor. And I guess the Nuns were mean as hell to Gwen and her younger siblings because they were racist and didn't like Vietnamese all that much.

So teenage time came around, and Gwen started dating gang members of the 5T. A gang whose name was three Vietnamese words that begin with the letter T. Which when translated to English means, "Childhood without Love." In fact, Gwen, at the age of 16 or seventeen, got the 5T tattoo on her right shoulder to prove she was one of the gang's girls.

Gwen showed me what the tattoo looked like before she had it covered with a devil tattoo so no one would ever know she was ever a part of it. This was also the same gang that got Gwen's baby brothers hooked on heroin so bad they both ended up homeless a few times. And in order to leave the 5T group and not be a 5T gang member girlfriend anymore, Gwen had to get passed around one night to a few of its members.

The reason why Gwen didn't want to date any of the gang members anymore is I guess the main leader died. And when he did, the gang started killing each other for who was going to be the new gang leader. And Gwen didn't want to die.

I find this weird too as Gwen's sister's boyfriend used to run with some biker gang called The Comanchero as he is best friends with one of its leaders. I feel like a dumb ass. Both those women ran to gang drug life because their real home life sucked.

The baby brothers whom they loved both get hooked on heroin because of it, which they both feel deeply guilty over. And since no one taught them what real love was, no wonder they both ran to evil men, drugs, and party nightlife. They had a lifetime of being used and abused long before I entered the picture, and I barely understand this now.

I was just thinking back then, ok, so you used to run with bad gangs; your past is your past. In reality, Gwen's past also shaped her future and how she took on relationships. Holy fuck, I am probably the only man who never hit her or used drugs or alcohol to take her to bed. I was the thing she had never experienced.

For what it's worth now, I pray Gwen finally creates a successful business and that the new love of her life makes her feel amazing.

Also, in case you are right about words, and actions finding their way to the people we desire most, and that this therapy becomes a book, and in the act of God, does fall into Gwen's hands?

Gwen,

Even though I may not cry with you or laugh with you or kiss you, I love you.

Chapter 17

"Sharing Stories"

The garden was warm this morning as I entered it, and Dr. Remy was just sitting there drinking hot coffee. For the life of me, I don't see how people can drink hot coffee on warm mornings. I sat down across from her and let our therapy session begin.

"Cliff," Dr. Remy said, "we should be celebrating your breakthrough. Great writing, by the way."

"I am trying," I said

"Your hooker story had me laughing pretty hard," Dr. Remy admitted, "a great way to use the name Charlotte to hide your friend's identity and foreshadow what was going to happen. Charlotte's web, she was a spider, spiders lay traps for their prey that look pretty until the horror happens. Fancy house with fancy glasses that serves cheap brandy? How much of that story was true, and how much did you take an artistic license?"

"Oh, that story was 98% true," I admitted to her, "I can't believe we acted like teenagers planning a keg stand about it, and it blew up in our faces. I just changed people's names."

We both cracked up about it because my life story was absurd and funny.

"Beside Gwen being bi-curious, did she ever admit to you why she wanted to try a threesome with you?" asked Dr. Remy

"No, she never did," I admitted

"You sound excited. Were you looking forward to this therapy session?" Dr. Remy asked

"Yes," I admitted, "I know it's going to be hard, but I know I am finally viewing Gwen in the proper light and her demons in the proper dark."

"So, I guess it is my turn for confession, huh priest?" Dr. Remy joked

"Yup," I said

Then I paused and let it set in. Dr. Remy knew something about me I hardly told folks.

"How did you know I went to seminary?" I asked

"I looked up your school transcripts from the VA records system to learn more about you," Dr. Remy said, "You started in Moreno Valley college, then transferred to a Catholic seminary. You didn't stay long, and my theory after reading your story so far, you love women. So celibacy for you is not an option you were going to take. You served in the Army used their tuition assistance program to gain a degree in philosophy. However, you never tell people you applied to a Baptist seminary in Virginia and got a master's in theology. While studying there, however, a more charismatic Christian faith gave you an honorary doctorate in divinity. You are way more educated than you allow people to believe."

"It's spot on, your theory," I replied.

"Well, the more pieces of a person I have, the more they are correct," Dr. Remy said, "I mean, I said Gwen could have turned to the Muslim faith based on what you have told me, and after reading the trauma's of Gwen's childhood and being involved with countless men who used and abused her? This is probably why Gwen's sexual activity is so risky and why sex for her at times can be meaningless. Just fucking someone is a whole lot different than making love to someone."

"True," I admitted, "Gwen even told me sometimes about why she was able to move on from someone, was to get under someone."

"So now knowing your personal history more in-depth," said Dr. Remy, "I now see why your writing therapy reads like a modern version of "Dante's Inferno." A holy man goes to hell, where it's cold, and his savior Christ is a burning fire. Gwen is your flame, and this facility, and your life after her, is a torturous hell without her. You write me like Dante's guide in hell. Helping you make sense of your world and make sense of Gwen so that you can forgive properly. Yet, you write it under the guise of the story structure of "Interview With the Vampire." We have our therapy sessions, and you tell your story, your truth, just like exactly how the interview book is written. And like a vampire creates another vampire, an addict can break someone and create another addict. And you hate your addiction like Louie hates being a vampire. Vampires like addicts suck the life out of people around them, which is why you quoted V for vendetta as your closing statement to Gwen. The statement comes from a woman trapped in a prison talking to another woman trapped in a prison. An addiction is a dark prison that is hard to escape. Yet, you love Gwen deeply, though you hate to admit it."

"I feel you have a hesitation in your voice, doc'," I told Dr. Remy as she paused and weirdly looked at me as if to study me and held something back that she wanted to say.

"Cliff, the story I have to share," Dr.Remy said, "in order for you to open up about your daughter, though I have shared it a thousand times, is a hard story to share."

"Doc', I told her, "we got all the time in the world."

"You quote the Bible's wisdom books when you talk, but in modern English," Dr. Remy said, "why are they your favorite books in the bible?"

"Proverbs is written like a wise teacher hoping their students adhere to basic principles of life," I said, " The book of Ecclesiastes is of a bitter old person seeing that wisdom sometimes doesn't guarantee a good life as goodwill suffer, and evil will prosper at many times. The book of Job teaches us that pain is inevitable and no one will ever have the answers to why human beings will suffer periodically."

"You memorized those books, didn't you?" Dr. Remy asked

"In my own way, yes," I admitted.

"Interesting," Dr. Remy replied, " Now it's my storytime."

Dr. Remy paused for a good long while as she quietly sipped her coffee.

"Do you want to know a taboo thing about rehab places?" Dr. Remy asked

"Sure," I said

"Because of how much we councilors, therapists, and psychologists, get to know truly intimate details of patients' lives," said Dr. Remy, " and patients feel heard and respected so much that at times inappropriate relationships do transpire between patient and doctor."

"I don't care if you slept with a patient doc'," I said

"Just give me a moment," said Dr. Remy as she held one finger up as a way to silence me.

"It was the spring of summer in 79 Rochester, New York. The summer had not come yet, and the morning cold had faded. Back then, it was ok for a 16-year-old to be dating a 20-year-old, and no one would bat an eyelash. Especially if the two lovers were minorities as we were. I won't share his name, but he definitely shared my youthful lust. We were two kids walking on the dying hippie movement and at the cusp of consumer excess that was the 80s. But, he and I were inseparable," Dr. Remy told me.

"He was your Gwen," I assumed

"Yes, he was very much my Gwen," Dr. Remy replied, "We found out using heroin together was a beautiful, safe haven for outcasts like us. We smoked it and shot it. Before long, our safe haven became the stuff of nightmares. I ended up turning tricks three to four times a day to get a new fix for us, and he would give tricks for the gay men in our area. One night, when I overdosed, he was nowhere to be found because he was servicing a man in a porn theater when those still existed. He got arrested and was sentenced to six months for lude behavior. He never made it out of jail, though."

"Wait, why?" I asked

"Because it was the time where the Aides scare began in America," Dr. Remy said, "and because his lude act was caught with a man, the other men he shared jail time with beat him to death in his own cell. I, on the other hand, after my overdose, was sent to court-appointed rehab, where I met and fell in love with my husband."

Dr. Remy sipped her cup of coffee again and paused before continuing as if she was careful with choosing which worlds to convey her story.

"I was the aggressor towards him," Dr. Remy said, "within months of getting clean and using my ex's life insurance policy to go to college, I pursued my husband for two years. Then he finally let up and agreed to take me on a date."

"What happened next, had a bad date or something?" I asked with a slight grin

"No," Dr. Remy said laughing, "I fucked the hell out of him and never left his apartment."

We both laughed at this small pause in Dr. Remy's story because most who meet her now just see a proper old Indian woman who's accent has slowly faded due to living in America too long and would never believe such a thing happened in her life.

"Well. I did leave for a brief moment to get us a bag of tacos and a couple of cokes," Dr. Remy admitted, "as my husband was like most bachelors, no food in the fridge but a lot of take out food bags in his trash can."

"Lucky guy," I laughed

"Oh please, I was a God sent in that day and age," Dr. Remy said, "giving a man a blow job at that time was considered whore like behavior, and not many women wore thong underwear. If women did wear thongs, it was for bedroom purposes only. Not like now, where women everywhere enjoy them as normal attire. So me wearing a thong and blowing him, I was the only girl he was going to have that was give him a good sex life."

"Huh, I forgot about that," I said, agreeing, "we only been more sexually open in society in the last 20 to 30 years."

"That's why I used to joke with my clients," said Dr. Remy, "all it took for me to get my husband was two years of stalking and a blow job. Then he took me down the aisle in Vegas two weeks later."

I couldn't help but laugh at the thought of what was going on. I am sitting down in a garden that looks like Heaven itself created it and listening to a proper and well-mannered elderly lady talk dirty. Trust me; the irony was not lost on me.

"Well, nice to know what underwear my shrink wears," I joked back, confirming I was ok with off-color humor.

"Oh no, honey, my ass sags too much now to wear those things anymore," Dr. Remy said with a poise that made me laugh harder, "my husband got all his goodies when his pencil worked; I don't need to do anything now. He's locked for life."

"Wait, I thought you guys were only married for 25 years?" I asked confused

"Yes, your American country is quite weird," said Dr. Remy, "Some American states don't view marriage in other countries as valid. So, technically I had three marriages with my husband, and only 25 years of it, according to American documentation, actually counted. Thank God those stupid laws were changed, but of course only after we did exactly what the tax court document said what to do."

"Yeah, the laws in this country are a bit slow in the change department," I admitted before jokingly asking her, "So, since you got married three times, does that mean if you two were ever to divorce, you'd have to go to divorce court three times?"

"Please, if he'd ever want to divorce me, this is America," said Dr. Remy, very dry, "I'd just shoot him. Bullets are cheaper than paperwork."

Hearing this dark joke from Dr. Remy, with such deadpan delivery, had me laughing so hard. It took me a good minute to stop.

"It is still hard for me to admit to people," said Dr. Remy in all seriousness, "that my dear sweet husband's wife is an addict. Just because I no longer use or have the cravings, I know the lifestyle I lived prior to him was dangerous and could have gotten us both sick in the long run. But it didn't. I never contracted aids or any other STI's."

"So, you are his Gwen," I said as everything she was telling me sank in

"Yes," Dr. Remy said, "addicts can change. But who they change for is only one person. I had to find myself to change, and my husband became the pursuit to stay clean because my heart fell deeply in love with him. So, here is where I give a piece of hope to your heart. Maybe Gwen did find that love worth pursuing that keeps her clean, and in the process found her true self."

"Thanks doc', I needed that," I admitted

"I know," Dr. Remy replied, "and now to talk with you about your other issues with Gwen. The reason Gwen enjoyed such taboo sex with you, wasn't cause of her drug use. Yes, addicts can become dangerously promiscuous, where they can have multiple partners without using protection. But there's something more to Gwen's wild side that you are not seeing."

"Which is?" I asked

"True love," Dr. Remy said, "during her time with you Gwen fought hard to stay sober, and shared her bondage sexual nature because you focused on her needs, wants, and desires. You never judged her, and you paid attention in how she needed this sexual freedom, where she didn't feel used like a human toilet. Again, you are very good at actively listening to your lovers. A gentle lover in a hard shell. Which is why, the frequency of the sex with her probably was a lot, and why certain kinky things she wanted to do slowly began to calm down to a pace you could handle."

"I never thought about that," I admitted, "Because during the sober months on my off time, and her off time, we had sex, 3-5 times a day. The hardcore kinky stuff that made me uncomfortable never got brought up, and the limits I was ok with, Gwen made sure to do them most often. I still think she over played it a bit, as used to say she was craving to give me a blow job over the phone, or sneak me away from visiting people to give me a taste of one. One time Gwen even went overboard with it as I was helping her on her farm in her greenhouse. She pulled my pants down out of nowhere and started giving me one out of nowhere, and we almost got caught by her two boys."

"That was probably real, Cliff. Because that sounds like a woman, who only knows men want sex, and she fell deeply in love with you, so she was giving her heart through her body because that is all she knew how to do. Of course you didn't see this, your anger with her ran deep," Dr. Remy said, "life for Gwen must have been hell at times. Growing up in a country that made her feel unwanted after an unpopular war ended. Being told what a woman is, how a woman should act, and what a proper marriage life and sex life should be, yet, knowing she was different. Being judged harsh for not being white. Getting involved with bad men who abused her. Then, when she grew up, she then craved sex in unconventional ways that were not popular ideas when growing up. Then here you come, and make life worth it. You were the bull in the china shop of Gwen's life. She was trying to make sense of you, and why the hell her heart fell so hard for you. Which means in an unhealthy used sex as way to make you stay, becuase fear of losing you was real. Which makes more sense. Now that I think more on Gwen's past with you."

"What makes you say that doc'?" I asked

"Gwen cried when you made love to her after she messed up, made her feel human," Dr. Remy said, "you didn't yell at her, you didn't stir a fight. You gave her genuine love from your soul. That moment meant everything to her. And it is that moment that will confuse her about you for the rest of her life."

"Just like I am confused about her," I admitted,

"Like I said, you loved Gwen with a love woman around the world wish they could feel," said Dr. Remy, "but sadly you weren't prepared for a dark addiction that kept Gwen from ever giving that love back properly. As we talk about this, you come to a deeper understanding of Vickie?"

"Starting to," I admitted

"Good. It's hard to forgive people who wronged us for no reason," Dr. Remy said, "but understanding her mentality will help you understand Gwen's addiction even more. Like I told you, normal people who love an addict can become controlling, manipulative or liars towards the addict, because they are trying everything within their human nature to save the addict. It's possible you gave Vickie anxiety that turned to rage, because your love affair with Gwen started out like a thousand other meaningless love relationships in Gwen's life."

"She did try moving Gwen from out of the city onto that farm," I admitted, "and got her to go to a meditation retreat."

"But Gwen hid the fact that she was still using it from her sister," said Dr. Remy, "so when Gwen's naked photos got found out, and your love affair became more public, you were the reason and the purpose, why Gwen went back to partying, even though Gwen fibbed to her sister by not admitting the truth, she was still using. There is a reason why ALONON therapy exists, for those recovering from loving a drug addict."

"I was a symbol of Gwen's addiction, Vickie could punch," I said

"A tool to be used for Gwen to hopefully wake up and change the patterns of her life," said Dr, Remy, "and the more you two fell in love, the more Vickie lost that control of trying to save her sister."

"So what do you really think happened after me doc'?" I asked, "And I get you letting me know Gwen might have created a good life now, but what is your true theory?"

"Did Gwen move from out of the city before the farm house?" Dr. Remy asked

"Yes," I replied

"And Gwen had other lovers besides her children's father?" Dr. Remy asked

"Yes," I replied

"And Gwen started businesses too, in the past, right?" asked Dr. Remy

"They would've sold the house and Gwen would try to restart somewhere else again," I said, "like a tired old broken record."

"An addict can restart their lives a thousand and one times, but if they don't fix their core issues," Dr. Remy said, "and understand why they are so self polluted with their issues that they become toxic to their own life, their broken life gets stuck on repeat."

Therapy with Dr. Remy was sinking deeper and deeper into my soul, as the truth of Gwen was coming to the surface from underneath all my emotional baggage.

"So don't be hopeful for Gwen, yet?" I asked Dr. Remy

"Oh no, I definitely have hope for you to think on. Gwen is going to crave you or something like you two had that hopefully will get her to chase a new life," said Dr, Remy, "however, I need to ask. Did Gwen ever get to meet Sam?"

"No," I said, "after Gwen really hurt me on the one drug binge that I tried to commit suicide over, I changed plans for Sam to not meet her unless Gwen was to get clean. Had my sister call and lie, saying Sam got sick and couldn't fly in to visit us."

"To protect your daughter from a possible bad love," said Dr. Remy, "you manipulated and lied to Gwen because in your soul you knew Gwen might be a bad experience for her."

"Because those of us who love addicts pick up bad traits in an attempt to save them, and protect others we love, from the addict," I said as therapy now was fully clicking in my brain.

"Which is why Gwen went on a binge the day of your daughter's funeral," said Dr. Remy, "in Gwen's eyes she was going to have a step daughter from her husband, and now that dream came crashing down."

"She needed to pop," I said

"And in your worldview, Gwen desecrated the most sacred thing in your life," Dr. Remy said, "so the rage you had over your daughters death, and those actually responsible for your daughters death, Gwen became the symbol of. Because your daughter was killed in a car accident by a truck driver high on drugs, and alcohol. And you knew Gwen drove intoxicated many times."

"I did to Gwen, what Vickie did to me," I admitted as more things came to light

"We learn the most from the people who impact our life the greatest," Dr. Remy said, "which is why I always say, show me your friends and I will show you your future. There are things we learn from other human beings we are unaware of until it happens. Vickie didn't want to hurt her sister, unfortunately Vickie didn't learn what you are learning now. And Vickie in some ways will always be an unintentional catalyst for Gwen staying stuck in her addiction cycle."

"Fuck. This shit hits hard doc'," I admitted

"I do think though, you were right about Vickie's book," Dr. Remy said, "the child development timeline and the story told in her book, don't match up. Doesn't mean she wasn't told stories from friends and relatives about the collective trauma the family went through. This comes even more apparent as the book only has a best seller sticker, and no other huge awards from well respected establishments like the Hugo award, or a Pulitzer. Big organizations make sure stories are authentic in peer review with deep scrutiny, before giving a prestigious honor to a book. Plus the best seller mark on her book, doesn't mean a million copies sold, it just means she met a quota needed for that branding."

"So why would she write a book about a family's collective trauma, and sell it as her story?" I asked confused

"Because it's still the truth, even though wrapped in a fib," Dr. Remy said, "the horrors to her family still happened, and she had to grow up around it. And her book does shine truths about the Vietnam war that otherwise would have gotten lost."

"So you don't think she tried to do it for fame?" I asked

"Oh she definitely did it for fame," Dr. Remy said, "no one writes a book and tries to make it on Ted Talks, if they don't want to be famous no matter how many times they deny it. And that's perfectly normal and human."

"You are stopping me from using Vickie's interference as a punching bag as part of the reason why Gwen and I broke up," I said as my brain was connecting the dots.

"Yes, because it is easy to do in the aftermath of things," Dr. Remy said, "Though Vickie treated you horribly and villainized you, it is easy to do in return, instead of turning the cheek."

"I thought we were gonna go deeper with things about my daughter?" I asked

"Don't need to," Dr. Remy replied, "you hiding your daughter from your therapy is in a way of you hiding your daughter from Gwen after Gwen went on a bender. So we need to fix the broken parts from you first that Gwen left you, and when you go through trauma therapy in 6 months with your other doctor, it would be wiser to explore it then."

"Then what are we doing now?" I asked

"Saving your life," Dr. Remy replied, "you cut yourself off from the world and blitzed yourself every night hoping to God you'd wind up dead. I am here reminding you, you are worth loving. Because I know from your educated background you figured out how Gwen's toxic lifestyle broke you, and in return didn't want to break anyone else. So you would rather die alone, then make another monster."

"Fuck, you're good," I admitted as I wiped the tear from my eye, cause Dr. Remy was right.

"I've been doing this for a minute," Dr. Remy said with a smile, "so, proving to you that you deserve love, I am going to have you show yourself in another "chapter"."

"Ok," I agreed

"No doubt Gwen adored you, and you would have given you anything if you asked," Dr. Remy said, "give me two stories where Gwen focuses on you, where you know deep down, Gwen made you a king above all other men in her life. Because even though, that yes she cheated on you, and lied to herself and you about it when she was high, when she was sober? When was she really Gwen? Gwen worshipped you."

"How do you know Gwen worshiped me, and I wasn't just an emotional filler?" I asked genuinely

"She called you on blocked numbers checking in on you for a while after the break up," Dr. Remy said, "which is why I opened up with giving you hope about Gwen. It is highly possible you were her rock bottom for her to finally change. Unless the same people did the same things they always do, when Gwen's life falls apart. Then you were just another cycle for her to go through."

"But if I was just another cycle to go through, isn't it possible she didn't love me?" I asked

"Again, a woman doesn't tattoo her ass with your name," said Dr. Remy with a gentle laugh, "an area you find most attractive to her, unless she is making the statement that you own it. Yes, I figured out you are an ass man. It wasn't hard to deduce. The pantie photos, and you highlighting her panties were thongs, and g strings, was a dead give away."

"Smart one doc'," I said

"Like I said, been doing this for a minute," Dr. Remy replied, "so share when she made you King. Go deep into it."

"Ok, doc' I will after you answer me this first though," I said

"What?" she asked

"Why are you having me explore my deep sexual relationship so much when it comes to Gwen?" I asked

"You are ready to know now, I guess," Dr. Remy answered, " I am getting you ready for your therapy you will undergo in the coming months. It has the highest success rate of curing alcoholism, and post traumatic stress disorder."

"Which is?" I asked

"MDM cognitive therapy," said Dr. Remy

"Ecstasy?!" I asked in shock

"Yes, in low doses though," Dr. Remy replied, "by doing therapy this way, getting you to write about your sexual adventures with Gwen, and getting you to accept your unique sexual lifestyl instead of crucifying yourself over it, I am creating new pathways in your brain that MDMA cognitive therapy will work. Because MDMA makes your brain and body feel as if you are having really good sex, and when you talk about your trauma and analyze your behaviors associated with that trauma, your brain then processes what happens and stops ptsd symptoms and alcoholic behavior."

"You mean to tell me, by me exploring my kinky sex life I explored wih my ex, is restoring me back to a normal human being?" I asked in shock

"Yes," Dr. Remy said, "people who survive trauma usually end up with a high sex drive, or sexual appitite. For years, doctors wondered as to why. It's not until we found out that MDM cognitive therapy cured PTSD and drinking disorders, that we understood why. The chemicals released during really good sex are healing to the human body. So a person having a hyper sexual life after a traumatic experience, in theory, is the human body trying to heal itself naturally with its own chemical compounds. They are also the same chemicals released in a child's brain when a mother is coddling them after they are scared, hurt, or angry. The human body and brain know what is needed to fix them at some level of consciousness, it just doesn't know how to get it."

"Which is why you pointed out before, there are so many bars, strip clubs, and brothels outside military bases around the world," I said, "trauma is good business to exploit."

"If there is a bad want or need, evil men will make a dollar off of it," replied Dr. Remy. "It is also why I view addiction as chemical bonding. People need healthy connections in life to function properly. A job they enjoy, lovers they enjoy, and other relationships that make life worth living. We are by design social creatures. So, for someone to fall into addiction after a huge traumatic event, or feeling empty because certain connections in life feel meaningless, the addict needs to be connected to a comforting source. Chemical dependency is the equivalent of a crying child being cared for by 1,000 mothers all at once. Which is why to a broken human being, it feels so right to chase the high."

Honestly, this was wild for me to hear, and even more wild after reading books and studies on this new therapy I was doing with Dr. Remy, I found more and more shocking. So, I guess the chapter, I will explore why Gwen made me king.

The song I listened to as I wrote this:

"I wish I was cold as stone

Then I wouldn't feel anything

Wish I didn't have this heart

Then I wouldn't know the sting of the rain

I could stand strong and still

Watching you walking away

I wouldn't hurt like this

I wish I was cold as stone"
Lady A "Cold As Stone"

Chapter 18

"A Man Made King"

The last therapy session makes this chapter somewhat hard to write. As things come more and more into a realization to me about Gwen, my heart finds more profound compassion that I never thought I would have for her. Seeing the world through a new set of eyes has allowed me to release hurt and anger at Gwen in a massive way.

Tonight on my phone, I watched a documentary on my cell phone called "Once Upon A Time in Cabramatta." Gwen talked about it with me before during our many long talks over the phone, and we even agreed we would watch the film together. Sadly we never got to watch it as planned. So tonight, in honor of what Gwen meant to me, I finally watched it.

My heart sank when I watched how a famous gang called the 5T's was a Vietnamese gang named for kids who knew no love. To grow up in a social climate where you are hated, your parents are overworked, and there's no real government help to help you transition into a new world you know nothing about must be really tough. I knew of the 5T gang stories through talking with Gwen's friends from time to time, but this definitely put it all in a new light. Yet it saddens me that stories like this will never stop until humankind stops having wars.

And this documentary shines a dark truth about war we never really think of as a species that we never take into consideration before any person picks up a rifle to go to war. We often just go with the mentality that a person sometimes has to act like a lion to be able to live as the lamb that they really are—forgetting one harsh truth that would stop any person from loading a bullet in a gun. It doesn't make a damned bit of difference who wins the war to someone who is dead. And yet an even sicker truth sinks into my belly, that only the dead have seen the end of war.

While fighting in Afghanistan, I saw more good come out of giving a poor man money and bags of rice than I saw me loading bullets in my rifle because every dead soldier was someone's: brother, sister, friend, lover, and so on, which made more people violent and looking for vengeance, and more dead bodies to be buried. Which is precisely why for myself, I will never own a firearm again. I refuse to be that close to death ever again in my short life.

I am not saying this life Gwen was born into gives a justification for her addiction and the self-destructive things it causes, but I am saying I understand it. Life can be cruel. For the world breaks everyone, and only the strong are found in the broken places. And those strong enough to survive the breaking can sometimes fall into the many poisons of life that slowly kill them as punishment for surviving; sex, gambling, drugs, alcohol. Life can beat one to their knees and keep them on their knees if a person lets it.

But the truly strong, the incomparable soul, are the saving graces to those who are lost. The addict that becomes the drug counselor or preacher that helps someone get on their feet. The sex worker who becomes a marriage therapist to help couples understand how to communicate appropriately so that the sex life is healthy and well balanced. Or the soldier who becomes the psychologist to help people grasp the realities of war.

I guess I really am a pacifist now. It only took rehab and therapy for me to accept this fact.

And all this is why, now understanding Gwen and myself further, I appreciate this story we lived. Love is a razor's edge of pain and pleasure. Both acceptance and the personal growth they pull out of you. Sometimes the keys to our future are in the stories of our lovers.

Also, I find it fitting I am writing these last chapters of my therapy to Tool's "The Pot." An anti-drug song the singer wrote for a friend dealing with heavy addictions issues. Which in itself is a testament I am seeing. Sometimes to love an addict pulls art from a wounded soul that connects with others in profound soothing ways. And so, on with the story, I guess.

One night, Gwen took me to King's Crossing. I don't know, someplace in the city. Apparently, this area was known for adult fun time stuff. Gwen and I took a taxi from the hotel we rented.

Gwen and I walked into a lover's shop to explore things that maybe we would want to play with or watch together. Like I said, after that moment her and I had at her house with the chain leash, our sex life was becoming more and more taboo for a while. Like Gwen sending me videos and photos of very risky outfits like a fishnet bodysuit that hid nothing and her playing with different toys. So, I was warming up to the idea of how far she wanted to push my sexual comfort zone. But I had to ask something that was on my mind.

"What did you really want to do if the threesome actually happened?" I asked her

"Everything you'd expect in a good porn," Gwen replied, "but that could be me romanticizing it a bit. You know why brothels have red lights, hubby?"

"No, why?" I asked

"To hide blemishes and wrinkles on the girl, to help make her more pretty," said Gwen

"Someone should have told that to the brothel we went to before Quasimodo stepped out," I joked,

Gwen hit me with a dildo that hung on the wall next to her in retaliation for my joke, playfully, of course. So I guess I can technically say I have been dick slapped.

Gwen checked her phone and noticed it was almost time for something,

"Time to go, hubby," Gwen said, "or we're going to miss your surprise."

Gwen then placed a scarf on my eyes and led me out of the store by the hand to a place that had loud music. Once we were inside, she took the scarf off my eyes, and I got to see she was taking me to a strip club.

"You said you never been to a strip club, hubby, and now you have," Gwen said with a huge smile on her face

I was half expecting a joke-like experience, but Gwen rented time with a gorgeous girl. And we followed her into a small private room. But as the show began to happen, Gwen noticed something. I didn't find the lap dance fun. The sex with Gwen was more than I had ever experienced with anyone, which made the strippers dance dull and pointless. That was until Gwen did something I didn't see coming.

Gwen began to dance with the girl and give me a show. Gwen and the girl would grind one another, and sensually touch each other slowly to the flow of the music's beat. Gwen made sure her eyes never moved off me, and made sure everything that she did while dancing with the woman was an erotic experience just for me.

When the song had ended, I just embraced in a kiss with Gwen and didn't pay the girl any attention after the show was done.

"Happy birthday, hubby," Gwen said

Gwen wrapped my arm around her neck, and placed her hand in my back pocket, and we both silently agreed we had enough of a strip show.

Just as we were about to leave the stripper stopped and chatted with us for a bit, and also talked some shit about other patrons at the club.

"So, how did you land an old school gentleman?" the stripper asked

"By being a lady in the streets, and the best damn thing he's ever had in the bedroom," Gwen said jokingly

"I wish more clients were like you two lovers," replied the stripper

"Why is that?" Gwen asked

"For the last hour before you came in for your appointment," said the stripper, "those drunk assholes have been asking to see my pussy, and being really sleazy."

"It's always some dumb dick head ruining fun nights," Gwen replied

"You have no idea, sweetheart," said the stripper, "say I got something for you two lovers if you don't mind humoring me."

Next thing I see is the stripper whispering something in Gwen's ear, and Gwen looked at me with a devilishly happy grin in her eyes as if her fire was being stroked.

Gwen led me to the bar, and ordered me a drink.

"Hubby, stay here for a second," Gwen said, "and whatever happens next, play along with it."

Gwen and the stipper disappeared for a breif moment, and when I tried to pay for my drink, the bartender didn't let me pay for it.

"Your money isn't good here sweetheart," the bartender said, "real gentlemen get treated well at my bar."

I watched as Gwen and the stripper she left with came back with her and two more strippers, and led us back into the VIP room, leaving no dancers on the floor.

Of course this pissed off the drunks that were harassing every girl in the joint, and they tried many times to get into the4 VIP room. Honestly nothing happened in the VIP room, just us and the strippers seeing drunk horny losers begging to see some of the entertainment that I apparently "stole away" into the VIP room.

Watching those jerks walk out of the strip club drunk and pissed, was classic. I still laugh about it when I think about it.

When we walked out of the VIP room as new customers were filtering into the establishment, everyone noticed me walking out with Gwen and an army of strippers.

Watching a bar give me a standing ovation as they thought I had a wild time in the VIP room, stroked my ego a bit. And Gwen played into it.

"Thank you for the fun ladies," Gwen said, "now it's time to take my hubby to bed."

"Want a souvenir," The main stripper asked

"Yeah," Gwen said

Then I watched Gwen in a very show like way, untie the stripper's g-string and then walked over to me to place it in my coat jacket.

"A party gift for later, hubby," Gwen said loud enough for the bar to hear

As we left and walked a few blocks down the street, I took the strippers g-string, and threw it in the trash.

"Good boy, hubby," said Gwen

The show that stroked my ego was over, and my respect remained in the utmost for Gwen. We might have a unique view on sex than most, but I would never dishonor her in anyway.

After I took my shower when we got to the hotel, I had to ask Gwen why she did it.

"A good man needs to be honored in public from time to time," she said, "I love you hubby."

"I love you too," I said back

And that night, was we explored the kinky sex Gwen wanted to try, I made sure I didn't orgasm, just her. Every time I was about to, I would stop, and just focus on Gwen's body in a different way. Which became a small thing I did for her after that, once in a while. This made Gwen curious though that night.

"Why do you do that hubby?" Gwen asked, "making sure you don't cum sometimes even though I do?"

"Because there are times I climax, and you don't," I told her, "no one else did this for you from time to time?"

"No," Gwen laughed, "which is why you got the treat at the strip club, and us trying to have a threesome. A true gentleman should always get treated well."

Funny how anger and rage cloud the memories or suppress memories of the good nature of a person or the good words that they once told you. I guess the song that fits this writing is Lady A's "We Own The Night".

"Tell me have you ever wanted Someone so bad it hurts? Your lips keep trying to speak but you can't find the words Well I had this dream once and I held it in my head She was the purest beauty But not the common kind She had a way about her That made you feel alive and for a moment

We made the world stand still"

Lady A "We Own The Night"

Chapter 19

"Forgiving Us"

I didn't write another chapter on Gwen before this morning's therapy session, as I didn't need to. So, when I went to therapy in the Garden with Dr. Remy, her gentle smile confirmed what I already knew. My time with forgiving Gwen, forgiving myself, and therapy with Dr. Remy was coming to a close.

"You felt it didn't you, which is why you couldn't write more of Gwen?" Dr. Remy asked

"Yeah. It was like a ball of something negative released, very weird," I admitted.

"Happens when you realize how much a loved one actually invests in you,"said Dr. Remy, "when you realize in their own way, they wanted to keep you forever. Though they knew deep down, they couldn't."

"Also humbling me in the process," I replied

"You Americans have a deep sense of pride for sure," Dr. Remy laughed

"Am I always going to miss her this much?" I asked

"For you, yes," said Dr. Remy, "your love was real, Cliff. Gwen was to you, a wife, a lover, and the person who showed you part of yourself you didn't want to admit to."

"I from time to time look at the set of photos we took together, when we first met, and one photo from our time at the beach in Hawaii," I admitted to

"And no matter how hard you try, you can't delete them or look at them too long," Dr. Remy said

"Yeah," I admitted, "I don't want to forget her, and my heart knows it can't invest in another person, while she still haunts my heart."

"Bereavement," said Dr. Remy

"What?" I asked

"What you are feeling is a true love lost," said Dr. Remy, "people who divorce, have a loved one die, or in your case, a once in a lifetime true love end, you'll need your time to reset."

"You know when I wrote the last story of Gwen," I said, "I rushed the end a bit."

"I know," Dr. Remy said, "it reads as such. When you came to the realization Gwen was going to make herself look like a fool for you, and make you like a God amongst men, your heart realized her love was real. Though she did a lot to mortally hurt you, Gwen in her broken way, loved you deeply Cliff."

"Which is why you believe she too, thinks on me from time to time," I said

"How could she not, Cliff?" Dr. Remy asked, "She has to forgive herself for mistreating you when high on cocaine, lying to you about it, and forgive herself for missing your daughter's funeral that drove you to end your relationship horribly the wrong way."

"You know when we were on our way to ending our relationship as we tried working through Gwen missing my daughters funeral," I said, "there was a night, she didn't answer my phone calls for two hours. Just like when she would do when on a coke binge. So, being scared I called the cops to check up on her, and after the cops left, she finally called me back."

"And, what happened?" Dr. Remy asked

"Gwen said her neighbour Molly came over, and they shared a bottle of wine," I said, "guess Molly had been really stressed. But before all that, Gwen said, a real estate person was going to check on her house to make sure something was up to code."

"Ok, I am not following," Dr. Remy said

"When the cops called me back, they said our family friend was leaving," I told Dr. Remy, "and in a not so subtle way, confirmed Gwen was visiting a man before the cop made a house visit."

"So what happened next?" Dr. Remy asked

"I was going to let it go, and trust he met with a friend and didn't want to make things worse between us," I said, "Gwen had many guy friends and didn't sleep with them. But one day on a long phone call with her, Gwen was going to see her doctor. As she went into the doctor's room, I said goodbye and thought I hung up on her, and I didn't. I placed my phone on my kitchen counter, went outside, and did a few chores."

"And when you got back to the phone, you realized it was still on," Dr. Remy said

"Yes," I admitted, "and I over heard Gwen confess to her doctor she had sex with a man three days prior unprotected, and needed to get checked. That only confirmed my rage that Gwen didn't respect me or my daughter's death."

"The final straw," Dr. Remy said,

"Why did I overreact so badly when I found this out?" I asked Dr. Remy, "I reported to the cops what she had been doing with drugs, I ratted her sister out for cheating on her boyfriend, and told everyone the truth of what Gwen did to me and others."

"A crime of passion, Cliff," said Dr. Remy, "when a person is in love with someone, and the person cheats on them with no substance and of their own free will, the person cheated on can react with a moment of passionate rage. That can keep going and consume the person, until the cheater is mortally wounded. Can I give you comfort?"

"Yeah, of course," I said

"It's very clear Gwen relapsed when your daughter passed as a way to cope with her passing, she was going to be a stepmom after all," Dr. Remy said, "and with that understanding, someone going to a doctor to check if they didn't catch a disease after sex right away after that sexual encounter happened, means they regret the sexual encounter and are scared. So Gwen probably hated it and really felt guilty when the cop showed up, and told you the lie. Gwen knew she was caught."

"And?" I asked

"And nothing. When an addict gets caught being evil, the shame and guilt that comes from it," Dr. Remy said, "can torment an addict and make them feel less human when alone."

"How is this a comfort doc'?" I asked

"Because that transgression, the one that made you pop, because everyone has a boiling point," said Dr. Remy, "was the addiction and not Gwen. The nature of Gwen when sober shows her worshiping you, honoring you in front of others, and the demon of her addiction wants to use her, abuse her, and leave her with less than nothing."

"Know the demon from the person," I replied

"Exactly," Dr. Remy said, "some days you will be good with it, other days it will be a struggle. But loving Gwen for who she is and not hating her for what her addiction drove her to do, is a must. Learn from her, and grow Cliff."

"You think I will ever see her again?" I asked Dr. Remy

"I think, maybe. Who's to say my dear Sir Lancelot," said Dr. Remy, "all I know is your holy grail moment is coming soon. When a good man fights hard for the love of his life, and loses, all I know is, God, this universe, has a way of putting things back in that person's favor in a mighty way. Fighting for love is never easy, win or lose. And because you lost in love, and suffered a time in hell for that love, a great thing is coming your way that you don't see coming."

"And what is that?" I asked

"A love worth living for," Dr. Remy said

"So when do I start this MDMA thing?" I asked

"Next week," Dr. Remy said, "from now on, leave Gwen's demon of addiction buried here in this garden to give your life a new start."

"That reminds me of something Grant Morrison once said. Everyone does magic all the time," I said, "In different ways. "Life" plus "Significance" equals magic. Changing a person's mind is a great miracle of God."

"And there is no greater significance than to love properly," Dr. Remy said, "die on the cross of Gwen's sin, and forgive her like your God forgave you. Be for Gwen what no one ever has been, true love."

"Thanks doc'," I said with a smile, "I like that. Be true love."

"Good, let's go get some lunch," Dr. Remy said, "and maybe just maybe, you can explain something to me."

"Oh, what is that doc'?" I asked

"Why do you like Grant Morrison so much," Dr. Remy asked, "some of that man's books make no sense. I tried reading a few, and I felt I wasn't high enough to understand him."

And all I could do was laugh.

Chapter 20

"Redefining Love"

It was going to close with self recording my last therapy session with Dr. Remy, and leave my story open ended there. My therapy with Dr. Remy had concluded and I finally am on a healthy quest to forgive Gwen and myself, over the toxicity of our relationship. But fate had other ideas. Fate by the love of God, had thrown me a curve ball no one saw coming.

As I was sitting eating my lunch in the patient area, I was listening to "Wild, Wild, Horse," by Warren Zeiders and while doing so, I wrote a small love poem for Gwen as I couldn't take my eyes off of the photo I kept of her in my phone. I just simply wrote:

"I remember the first time I tasted your lips, when I held your hand and chased the sun. Wild were the thoughts of a boy becoming a man,

I wandered into your arms. Moments of bliss is all I have of you now, as time slowly fades away of what you were

But I will never forget such a sweet kiss, or how it felt to be alive in your ocean of sheets. Then the dawn came to whisk me away, and because of our beautiful night, I'll never be the same. Sweet memories of old hearts,

Confessions of a poet, in the dark."

And as I was feeling my spiritual high of poetry to Gwen, Dr. Remy sat across the lunch room table from me, and pulled out one of my ear buds.

"Hello, stranger," Dr. Remy said very cheeky, "is that poem for Gwen."

"It is," I admitted.

Dr. Remy took my small notepad I was supposed to be using for notes in my recovery classes, and yet here I was, writing a love poem to a woman who captured my soul.

"When the mood does strike you Cliff, you do write beautiful things," said Dr. Remy as she paused for a brief moment after reading my writing and looking at the photo of Gwen on my cell phone.

"Is this her?" Dr. Gwen asked as she pointed to my phone

"Yes," I replied as I watched Dr. Remy's eyes go somewhat blank. Like her eyes were holding information back from me, and didn't know if they should tell me something.

"Did you ever write something this beautiful to Gwen before?" Dr. Gwen asked, "and not for your blog. But something powerful and meaningful to her, and her alone?

"Yeah," I replied

"Show me?" asked Dr. Remy

As I unlocked my cell phone and turned off my music, and opened an email app I had not opened in a long, long time. I went to the emails I sent to Gwen, and picked the one email I sent to Gwen the one time I knew she turned drugs down in an effort to love me properly. I found it with ease as if God himself guided my hand to it. Once I found the email, I gave the cell phone to Dr. Remy to read it.

Needless to say Dr. Remy got teary eyed a bit when she this email:

"Damn you, you beautiful and loving woman. You have become something more to me than I could realize. It has been almost exactly one year since we sat at this email and wrote comforting words to each other after a night of blind passion. I don't know how or why it happened, I am just honored and humbled it did. I never knew after that email, after a few short months, you would become my wife. Again, I am humbled. Never in my life has someone put me so above them, and yet, here you are loving me without boundaries. Loving without care of what your family thinks or what your friends think of me. For this my beloved Gwen, I promise you this. My love, my loyalty, my respect, and friendship will always be yours. In my eyes you have become the greatest woman I have come to know and admire. A strong mother who provides and protects her boys like a magician. How you can take $20 dollars and stretch it into $100 dollars, is beyond me. I love how you grow healthy food for them on your farm, so they can have home grown food on their plates every night. And how you kiss them every night and make sure they both go to bed, and wake up with the first and last thing ever said from your lips, I love you.

I even felt it was heartwarming when your little one needed to sleep with his mommy after having a nightmare, and so we had to hang up from our nightly talk, only for you to text me like a teenager in the dark. Or at times you called me in the morning whispering cause the boys fell asleep with you in the bed as you guys were watching movies on your laptop. From where I am sitting, and seeing, you love them, and would do anything for those two boys.

But beyond this, I am proud of you baby. I am proud that you are trying to put your demons to rest. I have to come clean. I did want to run when I found out you struggled so deeply with cocaine addictions and a party life. I was scared. But I stayed. I stayed because you showed me who you are. I stayed cause I saw your true value. I get it, you enjoy kinky sex, and love stuff in the bedroom that makes most people uncomfortable, which why when you showed me the real you, I lowered my guard down, and explored that side of you. And after, I always made sure I made love to you, to make sure you knew, even if your kinky sex stuff stopped, I was going to love you until the day I died.

And when you stepped up to stop your party lifestyle for all of us: the boys, Rebel, me, and us…. OUR FAMILY. OUR future. You would think it would have been the tattoo, but the spiritual moment for me, was this moment. The moment when the person passed you the bag and you gave it back and you called me instead. It was a sucker punch to my heart. I wanted to reach through that phone in that moment, and kiss the ever loving hell out of you. Instead I went on an internet shopping spree for you and bought you that bluetooth thingy you love to hate.

I know when we first started I had 1,000 things batting against me, and recently, a million things were batting against you. But here we are.

Unafraid. Loving. Brave. I will be your armor and protect you from all the things you have done, as long as with every beat of my heart, your love is mine. And only mine.

And fuck people who don't understand our ten year age difference, or culture difference, and how they don't understand how two lovers from two different countries fell in love and live for each other unlike those poor bastards trapped in "conventional marriages". Though it was just a religious spiritual unity between us with no real paperwork, it is real to me. You are my wife. I love you, Gwen.

Sincerely,

Hubby."

Needless to say, I had to give Dr. Remy her moment, and grab a tissue to wipe her nose, and eyes.

"Proof,"Dr. Remy said, "that anger can poison the mind and ruin something so pure as gold. The old you saw, what you had to relearn here. So, when that anger comes, reach far back into that memory in your soul, and this young man, the young man who wrote these beautiful words to Gwen, let that young man remind you why he wrote them."

Dr. Remy had been right. Along the way of trying to save Gwen, I lost sight of the truth I already knew. Drugs make people into someone they don't want to be. Gwen loved her family dearly and wanted to be something more, but her addiction was the monster under the bed or in the closet, ready to pop out and destroy everything she held dear.

"Why are you crying over my email?" I asked

"Like I told you a million times before, Cliff," said Dr. Remy, "you loved Gwen with a love that makes women's hearts melt. You know how many lonely people in the world there are that are waiting for someone like you to drop into their lives, and love them like this?"

Dr. Remy held the phone up to me as to drive the point home further.

"I know I was selfish with my love for Gwen," I replied

"Of course you were selfish with it," Dr. Remy scoffed in a joking manner, "you would be a fool not to. You don't see it, but reading this, as a woman who has lived a very long time Cliff, and seen a world of things in my time? No woman ever, I don't care, could ever forget a love like this. This love you gave Gwen. It's the love that drives inspiration to write great romance novels that lonely lovers read on valentines day."

"Yeah," I kind of agreed

"You are one of those men who buys friends Valentine day gifts aren't you? said Dr. Remy

"Yeah I do," I admitted, " I don't like people feeling lonely or forgotten about, on a day where people are supposed to be thought about."

"Sweet as candy and dumb as an ox," Dr. Remy laughed, "the old woman bitch in me wants to smack you."

"Wait, why?" I laughed in return

"Do you understand the main theory that we people are attracted to others to form groups and unions with one another?" Dr. Remy said dismissing my request why she jokes about slapping me

"No," I said.

"Was as human beings are communal," Dr. Remy said, "we build community out of everything so we can belong to someone, or a group of people. This is why people connect over food, music, or a simple smoke during a fifteen minute break at work.Which is why, if your religions stories are true, why Jesus came down and ate with human beings. God himself came in the flesh to connect over simple meals, because He understood humans unlike humans understood themselves. Because God knew we were created in his image, so he knew how to connect us."

"Ok, that sounds fancy and all, but you don't believe in my God," I replied

"It doesn't matter, you do," said Dr. Remy, "And that makes all the difference."

"I get it, a higher power will lead me beyond my suffering," I said a little annoyed

And this, this was the point where the old lady bitch inside Dr. Remy finally slapped me. Which, for a sad choice of words, was a sobering experience. I let her have her moment, and breathe. Nor did I report what happened after the incident as I was trying to learn wisdom from a tired woman tired of repeating herself to broken people.

"Did you know for a brief season, schools in California showed students "A Knight's Tale," in English class," said Dr. Remy, "as to help students connect with "The Canterbury Tales" by Geoffrey Chaucer?"

"Yeah, that was my dumb ass generation," I said, "that story "A Knight's Tale", has nothing to do with Chaucer's short story in "The Canterbury Tales '. It's a poor boy dressing in fancy armor, and changing his destiny. The short story was wildly different. The movie painted Chaucer as a gambing drunken degenerate, that got stripped of his clothes for being unable to pay his debts."

"Stories are people connecting about things they are trying to make sense of," said Dr. Remy, "music for instance, is a story being told through poetic format, and driven by an arrangement of sounds that match the emotions of that story."

"Which is why Rap, and Country are the world's most popular genres," I replied.

"People have to connect," Dr. Remy said, "people need to belong to someone or something. Which is why we love our personal country over another. Or we choose our spiritual beliefs because we grew up in them from our families world view, because we want to belong to our families, or we abandon them as we make our own sense of what family is."

"Holy shit," I said, "You're an atheist. Then why pretend to practice your culture's spiritual beliefs?"

"To remind me not to be an asshole," said Dr. Remy, "I practice it to keep my mind open to other people. It helps me remember the core values of how to relate to a person. Just because I don't believe in it, doesn't mean I shouldn't practice it for the benefits of it's wisdom, and human connection."

"Because religion is another group of stories of a culture of people," I said, "trying to connect with the world. The bible I was told in seminary, was 90% storytelling, and 10% of people reacting to that long formatted story."

"Which is why human beings choose certain political beliefs, certain political parties," said Dr. Remy, " history is the world's longest story ever written. We live by the stories we experience, and by the stories we are raised with."

"No one human being is truly a loner as they need to connect with the world around them, " I replied

"Look at your country America for a second," said Dr. Remy, "people who studied politics, socialnomics, philosophy, and religion, are amazed at America's storytelling. America is the youngest nation, yet, America's created stories of legend from their historic heroes, and villains as if they lived 1,000years. But America is the world's youngest country."

"How does this connect with Gwen," I laughed

"You belong to a country of Misfits, outlaws, and outcasts," said Dr. Remy, "who got tired of playing by the world's rules and tried creating your own."

"Yet, we made the same mistakes of our predecessors," I replied.

"Because that is the story and influence you Americans come from," Dr. Remy replied, "though you rebelled against the British Crown, sometimes in History, America acted like the British Crown."

"You are puffing up my American pride while dismantling my beliefs of my country, why?" I asked

"To show you Gwen's life in a light you haven't thought of," Dr. Remy said

Then it hit me like a diesel truck smashing into a trailer home. I listened to Gwen's life story, but I did not pay attention to it.

"I am not done with my story of Gwen, am I?" I asked

"You are. You forgave Gwen," said Dr. Remy, "and learned tools to distinguish between Gwen, and her addiction. Plus, you are learning on how to forgive yourself on the whole Gwen love affair."

"So, what am I missing doc'?" I asked

"Understanding," replied Dr. Remy, "people fall in love with addicts because their personal stories connect, most of the time. Years ago, I helped a man in love with an Alcoholic woman. The man fell in love with a single mom with three kids. The man grew up with no dad as his father died before he was born, and was raised by a single mother. So the guy helped raise three kids, not his own, and yet, the woman drank herself slow. She drank so much she developed brain retardation. And He came to ALONON therapy to get help with his life."

"Gwen was a refugee of war, and I was a solider of war, so we connected on a deep level," I replied

"The deepest level. To connect on human tragedy is deeper than any connection known to humankind," Dr. Remy said, "you both in your own ways lived through war, and were left to deal with its aftermath. Lovers got married over less."

"Fuck," I replied as the documentary of Cabramatta hit hard as it finally told me the truth of Gwen's life, "Gwen and her friends grew up with and around the 5T's. Drug's, sex, and fuck you, is all she knew. This world didn't give her a home, a voice, or a place to belong. But drug culture did. Fuck. I am so fuckin' stupid."

"Don't," said Dr. Remy, "everyone has their own path. According to your spiritual Christian belief, God brought you into Gwen's life, lean into that."

I had to gather myself a bit and as I did, I realized Dr. Remy and I had been talking so long, lunch was over and the lunch room was empty. Signifying my true last therapy session with Dr. Remy only began in the Garden.

Chapter 21

"Understanding"

D r. Remy's words hit like a freight train on a cold windy night. A shock to the reality I put myself in, from the reality that actually lived. Sobriety can suck.

Gwen's real life experience tasted like a mouth full of salt to my pride. At times when Dr. Remy was talking, my self righteous indignation wanted to gag and make me suffer for being so ignorant. Now I really understood the literary character Mr. Darcy, the arrogant prick, from an unflattering life lesson. Not once did I listen to my sweet Gwen's life story as I listened to a wild lover. Tell them the right thing to get into their panties for the night. Yet, I confessed Gwen to be the greatest love of my life, and my heart tortured me for this truth, over and over and over, again. Love can be a painful lesson, I am now most assured.

"Trauma is a human connection most misunderstood," Dr. Remy

"It's because it's a truth the world hates to admit," I replied

"Did you really read Hemingway?" asked Dr. Remy

"Yes," I replied, "after the war, I read "A Farewell To Arms", with great fervour several times."

"Do you now understand the trope of a woman of light, and a woman of dark?" Dr. Remy asked

"yes," I replied, "to see the light in some people, we must first experience the dark to appreciate the light they try to share with the world. Which is probably why when Hemingway shot himself with a gun used in the

American civil war," I said, "his wife claimed it an accident from cleaning the gun, yet, the doctor presumed over his case, said it was suicide."

"In The Crow, James O'Barr cited a lot of Joy Division," said Dr. Remy, "loved how you used this trope of his and shared the music you listened to as you wrote. It gave your story a greater depth. As one can hear the songs and feel the emotions you had while writing each page."

"Ask what you are going to ask doc', don't beat around it," I requested

"Cliff," she asked with a shake, and tear in her voice, "was Gwen your other lover? Or your layover between flights from one lover to the next?"

These questions were like a kick in the teeth, and something I never gave thought to. I was always accused of this by Vickie, Gwen's sister, and here it is again, asked of me. It's almost like the world have made women cynical of men, and men burnt out of being real lovers due to this cynicism.

Gwen's sister's both ridiculed me, and villainized me in horrific ways in texts to Gwen. In fact one time, Gwen's younger sister (who was listening to Vickie), asked some messed up stuff about me in Vietnamese like:

"You sure he won't rape you?"

and "Are you sure I won't find your dead body in a dumpster?"

Worst part she did it right in front of me, and when she left, Gwen had told me what her younger sister said because she was being influenced by Vickie.

Then small alienating questions like if Gwen was my second lover or my lay over between love flings as I was 10 years younger. I don't know why the world breeds such dark views in folks but it does wear thin on a tired soul, I have to admit

So, I told Dr. Remy the truth.

"Never," I declared, "and those are questions like that, is why I began to resent Gwen's sisters. I only used the tropes you asked of, to help me separate between who Gwen was, and what her addiction was."

"I only ask Cliff, because people connect to certain lines of dialogue in songs, and stories, for a reason. And you do have a history of not opening up all the way. As your doctor, it is my duty to ask," said Dr. Remy

"We'll, it's that kind of questioning that has my soul weary," I admitted, "it almost feels as if as of good men are tortured for what evil men do. Everyone desires grace and mercy for themselves, and yet, never wants to give it. So, good men suffer for the evil few, to where—"

"Where good men just give up, and no longer try to be in the world of lovers and pursuits," said Dr. Remy.

"Yeah, exactly," I said, "why bother try being a good man in this world, if you are beaten, scorned and hated for other men's sins? I mean, I know Gwen had unfaithful lovers in the past, and so did her sisters, I just don't understand why I had to bear the wait of those mistakes?"

"It's because good men are the only ones with the strength to help a scorned woman believe in love again, Cliff," Dr. Rem replied, "Tell me something about Gwen that no one knows, that you keep as a keepsake."

"There are many to be honest," I admitted shylly, "She wanted to have sex on the beach in Hawaii, but we got interrupted by a homeless man, and the second time she tried, we were in the water. The water was so cold, I couldn't get it up. So we didn't have a Hollywood moment in Hawaii. But the thing I never shared with anyone, the cute thing I miss? When Gwen sleeps, she waits until you fall asleep first, and watches over you until you do. When you're dead asleep, then she sleeps. But can I share something funny about her that I oddly miss?"

"Please do," said Dr. Remy

"When she sleeps?" I said, "she farts in her sleep, and doesn't wake up."

Dr. remy started to laugh hysterically at this

"It's true," I said, "one morning she admitted to me that my body heat was too hot, and finally understood why I removed covers off my body in winter. It was because of this she woke up freezing from being wet, because my body heat made me sweat like a gushing fountain as we slept. So to remedy this, Gwen thought it best to start wearing a run suit to bed. No joke. So if I sweated during the night, the run suit would get wet, and Gwen didn't care. Summer months we slept with no blankets and the bedroom was made as an icebox by Gwen. So I was in heaven. And I in return told her the truth that she farts in her sleep."

"So, how did you find out she farted in her sleep?" Dr. remy asked while laughing

"I went to go pee one night," I said, " and I noticed mini me was hard as rock. I went pee, and thought she and I after could have a little midnight tango. But after I got back from the rest room, I hear the loudest fart come from that midget woman that should have made the blankets levitate, and Gwen did not wake up a damn bit."

Dr. Remy busted up laughing hard

"I am serious," I admitted, "after that, every night I slept next to her and had to wake up to pee, or get a drink of water. That woman made bowel movements that made God's thunder jealous. Best part, she never woke up, ever."

Dr. Remy was laughing so hard, she started to choke on her water and cough. Funny how real life stories make us laugh better than rehearsed jokes? Who knows.

"You're lying," Dr. Remy laughed

"Right hand to God," I admitted, "I even told her about it and gave her the joke nickname fart monkey."

Which made Dr. Remy laugh even more

"The odd stories that come from lovers," Dr. Remy, " they never cease to amuse me."

"Speaking of," I said as I pondered a thought off topic, "why don't the small odd things lovers do never make it into books or movies? Every relationship has an odd quirk or two. Yet love writers never show this with the characters they develop in love stories."

"Odd observations, Cliff," Dr. Remy said with a smile, "but an amusing one. So, back to our topic-"

"Yes," I replied

"You ever hear about the rat park experiment?" Dr. Remy asked

""No," I replied

"Oh good," Said Dr. Remy with a smile, "everything pop culture and society believes about addiction is wrong. It's all based on a wonky experiment done in the 1930's. A mouse was put in a cage and given two water bottles. One laced with cocaine, and one without. The mouse chose the laced cocaine water bottle 100% of the time. So entire generations grew up thinking if you use drugs once, you're hooked automatically. Even though peoples grandmothers went in for hip replacement surgery, and did not come out of surgery as heroin addicts. Or children as young as ten, coming out of surgery needing a fix so bad, that they started taking cocaine bumps near the playground slide."

"Is this also why some parents today still think drug dealers will give a drug to try, so they can get you hooked, and make you a long term client?" I asked

"As stupid as that is in our society, yes," Dr. Remy said, " because if drug dealers were giving stuff for free back in the day, I would have found them, and so would other addicts. So you do see the faulty results from this bad experiment, and how it's made generations of naive beliefs about addiction?"

"So what happened," I asked

"The Vietnam war," Dr. Remy replied, "a ton of military men got hooked on opium and heroin during deployments. So Uncle Sam and the media, we're scared that when these soldiers come home, we would have the streets littered with dope addicts. And the news media narrative around that time, kept telling every nation, if they fought in Vietnam, they're an addict."

"Which is why a lot of movies back in the 70's and 80's, depicted every soldier home from war as having drug issues," I said

"Exactly," Dr. Remy said, " but do you know what really happened? These soldiers quit over night when they got home. As if they never touched a drug in their life. Which then made people start asking deeper questions about addiction. And the experiment rat park was created. Instead of using one rat, the doctors used a ton of them. They also gave the rats loads of cheese, and mazes to go around in. It was rat heaven. Then the doctors then put the two water bottles in the cage, one laced with drugs, and the other just pure water. Almost all the rats didn't take the drug, except one or two of them. As long as the rats could eat cheese, have sex, and the freedom to do what they desired, no rat became addicted to the drug water bottle."

"It's the environment that keeps the addict addicted and why some people who used drugs before don't get addicted to them," I said

"Gwen grew up with an outlaw party scene in cabramatta," said Dr. Remy, "that was her cage. I don't doubt Vickie heard of the rat park experiment, and was trying to help move Gwen out of her cage. But Gwen willingly kept going back to her cage, even though she had a choice to leave it. Why do you think the soldiers once taken out of their war environment stopped using, but Gwen kept going back to her environment ?"

"All I can think of is freedom of choice," I said

"We'll, you're not wrong, but it's more than that." Dr. Remy said, "Gwen wasn't living a fulfilled life. A person must have a life they feel worth living before they stop trying to escape from it. A lost person with no real purpose, will always find a means of an exciting escape from a meaningless life."

"Damn," I said as Gwen made more sense to me than ever before.

"So when it came to you," Dr. Remy said, "Gwen was getting a life worth living. In fact, did she ever use what I call the baby voice, like making a child-like voice around you?"

"Yeah, actually," I said

"Women make a weird voice when actually in deep deep love with someone," said Dr. Remy, "and it's only used when they're alone with their lover."

"After doing something that made Gwen happy," I said, "Gwen would talk in a cute voice where she curled her tongue."

"Now you know for certain, Gwen truly loved you, Cliff," said Dr. Remy

This conversation helped me forgive and understand more, and gave me the proof my heart needed that Gwen did love me, and wanted me in her life.

"Cliff, can I request something from you," Dr. Remy requested, "can you meet me here tomorrow night, and take this tired old woman dancing?

"Yeah sure doc'," I agreed, "what kind of music do you feel?

"We'll dance country western," Dr. Remy said, "a small town's Lady's music. We'll bluetooth it from a cellphone to the hall speakers in here."

"Yes ma'am," I replied

"Eight Sharp," Dr. Remy said, " Don't be late. Oh, and wear something more flattering than sweatpants, trim your beard, and comb your hair instead of covering it with a hat."

"Yes ma'am," I obliged her. I didn't know what Dr. Remy had planned but I was going along with her usual remedy for curing lost causes like me. But something felt different than her normal hippie request. Like it was something that was going to change my life.

So I recorded this event like the last, and when I am done, will record the next few events no matter where they lead.

Chapter 22

"Saving a Life"

onight was the greatest night of my new found life. My soul is whole again. Not to get too far ahead now, sorry hands still shaking.

I did what Dr. Remy requested and cleaned up a bit. I even went to the facilities barber shop to get properly groomed. The barber cut my hair, and trimmed and put smooth beard oil on my beard. And for the first time in a long time, jeans instead of sweat pants, and wore actual shoes instead of flip flops or poor man slippers. For the first time, in a long time, I looked like the old me again.

Around 8, I made my way to the dinning hall, and I could hear country music playing faintly from behind it's doors. Outside the hall, I couldn't make out the song, but as soon as I stepped through the hall's dining doors, the song could be heard as clear as day. "Pink Houses," by John Melloncamp.

And there was Dr. Remy in all her hippie glory, just swaying back and forth to it in a modified two step rhythm.

"Good, you made it," said Dr. Remy when she saw that I showed up, "and I see you have taken proper self care."

"Yeah, been a while," I admitted, "face still feels a little cold after the trim up."

"Galaxy, play country music for Cliff," said Dr. Remy as she placed her hands properly on my shoulders, my hands went gently around her waist, and we began to two step to some old George Strait songs.

The music was slow and soothing, still I had no idea why Dr. Remy wanted to dance, but I learned to trust this crazy woman.

"You missed a deep connection between "A Knight's tale, and Chaucer's original works you know that right?" said Dr. Remy, "which I find odd as you are a deeply analytical person."

"Chaucer's book showed the unflattery side of Knighthood, and kings," I replied, "Heath Ledger's film was about a poor boy changing his stars, and winning the love of his life."

"In Chaucer's book, the Knight had to learn how to treat a woman properly after being humbled for long years by a witch," Dr. Remy said, "Will in the movie had to prove himself humble for the love of Jocelyn, and prove himself an honorable man to love only her and not pursue other women. In both stories there is a Man learning how to love a woman properly."

"You are right, I really did miss that deep connection," I said

"Yeah, and I am shocked as to why," said Dr. Remy, "I mean you picked up on Will not knowing about church customs as Will is a poor man, therefore, could never afford to pretend to be pious like the rich did in the days of Knighthood, yet you missed that connection entirely. You understood both stories mocked the rich and were rebellious middle fingers to their rule. And your poetic heart couldn't connect the most obvious of parts?"

"Some lesson's take a minute, I guess," I said

"Also, in both stories the woman got to choose which lover had the right to pursue her," Dr. Remy said

"Right because in both stories men were conquering women, not loving them," I replied, "and it wasn't until the Knight learned of what the love of a woman is, before being allowed to pursue, and sway the one they actually desire. Perhaps angels have no names, only beautiful faces."

"Close your eyes Sir Lancelot," said Dr. Remy, as she had us stop dancing. Then she went over to a table and picked up a black scarf used for holding a woman's hair up and placed it over my eyes. It smelled like coconut.

And I was standing there foolishly with a woman's scarf over my eyes, I began to smell the sweet smell of Chanel number 5. My legs went weak, and buckled to the floor. My hands began to shake, as my heart race with anxiety, and sadness all at once.

"Doc', I don't think I handle this therapy session," I choked out, as I began to feel my body slightly shake

"It's ok, Cliff," said Dr. Remy, "this is the holy grail moment your soul has been begging your God in the dark, for a very, very long time."

No sooner did those words leave Dr. Remy's mouth I felt the warmth of strong female hands grab my face in soft caressing touch that took the breath from my lungs. And with there strength pull my mouth into a kiss I could never forget. The taste and the warmth of the lover my heart wanted to call home. My body just gave out, and fell into the arms my soul longed to embrace.

I was to weak from this emotional excitement, that the hands that drew me in for the kiss, had to remove the scarf. It was my beloved Gwen, the only woman who ever meant a damn to me. Her eyes were still the same sweet amber brown, and you smile still consumed my soul. Hair had grown more grey than when I saw her last, but it fit the beauty of her cheeks.

All I could do is weep in my beloved arms, and be held by the woman I could only ever love.

"How is this possible," I asked in complete shock

"Fate hubby," said Gewn, "after I got clean in rehab, I started a veggie shop that supplied to hospitals and rehabs. I came here to sign a deal with this facility as our business is growing here, and back in Australia. Oh, how I prayed to see you again."

Gwen began to cry with tears of happiness like I had never seen before.

"To truly love, is to be divine," said Dr. Remy, "I had no idea you two were each other's lover until she and I began meeting for lunch breaks and she shared her story with me. Then when I saw the picture on your phone, I had to let her know you were here. Plus you kept calling her Gwen in your story to hide who she was."

"Second chances are love miracles to make things right, ' " said Gwen, "love does not have to make sense, it just has to make things right."

Where this story takes us, I don't know. But I can say this for certain, Gwen and I both found a life worth living.

Now this story can be true, who is to say. I mean in order to write a love story, one must live one first. Then again this could be just mad typing's of a writer over his morning coffee....

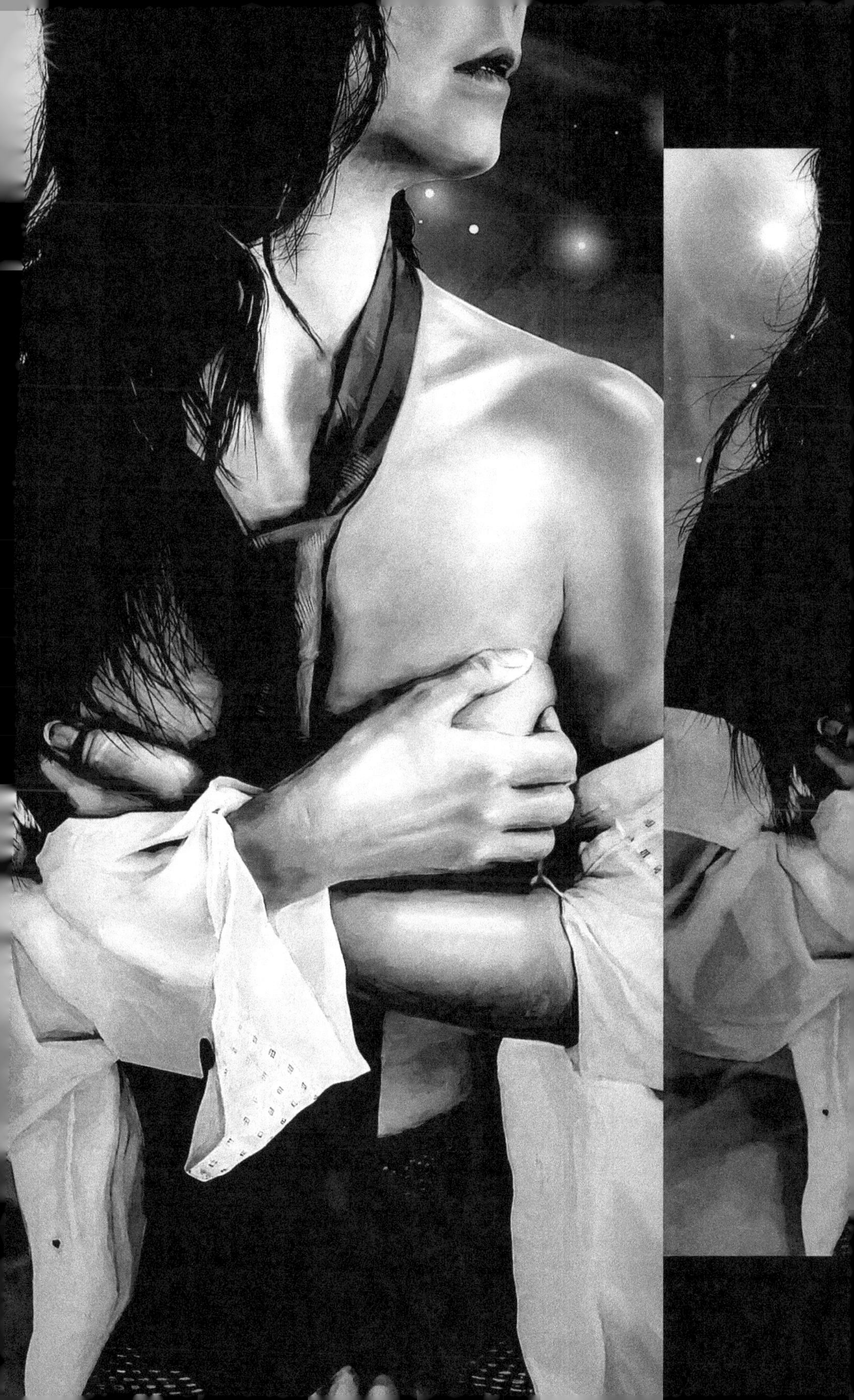